Best Bedtime Stories

Best Bedtime Stories

Adaptations by
Amy Friedman

Illustrated by
Jillian Hulme Gilliland

TORONTO   OXFORD   NEW YORK
OXFORD UNIVERSITY PRESS
1993

Oxford University Press, 70 Wynford Drive, Don Mills, Ontario M3C 1J9

Toronto   Oxford   New York   Delhi   Bombay   Calcutta   Madras   Karachi
Kuala Lumpur   Singapore   Hong Kong   Tokyo   Nairobi   Dar es Salaam
Cape Town   Melbourne   Auckland   Madrid
and associated companies in
Berlin   Ibadan

Canadian Cataloguing in Publication Data

Main entry under title:

Best bedtime stories

ISBN 0-19-540967-1

1. Children's stories. I. Friedman, Amy.

II. Gilliland, Jillian Hulme, 1943-

PZ5.Be 1993   808.8   C93-093690-6

Book design Kathryn Cole
Text copyright © Amy Friedman, 1993
Illustrations copyright © Jillian Hulme Gilliland, 1993
Oxford is a trademark of Oxford University Press

1 2 3 4 – 6 5 4 3
Printed in Mexico

For Alison, Brian, Cassandra, Gregory and Sarah
and with gratitude to
Neil, Norris and Maureen

Contents

◆

Acknowledgements

◆

Grateful acknowledgement is made to the following for permission to adapt or reprint their copyright material. Every reasonable effort has been taken to trace the ownership of all copyrighted stories included in this volume. The publishers will gladly receive information that will enable them to rectify any inadvertent errors or omissions in subsequent editions.

The Kingston Whig-Standard and the **Southam Newspaper Group** for granting permission to publish this collection from The Bedtime Story.

Adaptation of "The Thieving Dragon" by Kathleen Arnott from *Animal Folk Tales Around the World*, Blackie. Copyright © Kathleen Arnott, 1970.

Adaptation of "The Magic Brocade" by Eric and Nancy Protter from *Folk and Fairy Tales of Far Off-Lands*, Duell, Sloan and Pearce. Copyright © 1965 by Eric Protter and Nancy Protter. Used by permission of JCA Literacy Agency, Inc.

Adaptation of "The Tiger, the Brahman and the Jackal" from *Indian Fairy Tales*, edited and selected by Joseph Jacobs. New York: Dover Publications, Inc. Used by permission.

Adaptation of "The Dancing Stars" by Anne Rockwell from *The Dancing Stars*, New York: Thomas Crowell, 1972.

Adaptation of "The Lizard's Sorrow" by Mai Vo-Dinh from *The Toad Is the Emperor's Uncle, Animal Folktales from Viet-Nam*. Copyright © 1970 by Sung Ngo-Dinh.

"Talk" from *The Cow-Tail Switch*, by Harold Courlander and George Herzog, published by Henry Holt and Company, copyright 1947, copyright renewed 1974 by Harold Courlander.

Adaptation of "The Three Hares" by Margery Kent, from *Fairy Tales From Turkey*, Routledge & Kegan Paul, 1946.

Adaptation of "Mr. Lazybones," from *Floating Clouds, Floating Dreams* by I.K. Junne. Copyright © 1974 by I.K. Junne. Used by permission of Doubleday, a division of Bantam Doubleday Dell Publishing Group, Inc.

Adaptation of "Anansi Plays With Fire" by M.A. Jagendorf and R.S. Boggs from *The King of the Mountains: A Treasury of Latin American Folk Stories*. Copyright © 1960 by M.A. Jagendorf and R.S. Boggs. New York: The Vanguard Press, Inc.

Adaptation of "The Fool of the World and the Flying Ship" by Arthur Ransome from *Old Peter's Russian Tales*, Jonathan Cape, 1916. Permission granted by the author's estate.

"It Could Always Be Worse." Adapted from *A Treasury of Jewish Folklore* edited by Nathan Ausubel. Copyright © 1948, 1976 by Crown Publishers, Inc.

Adaptation of "How Brother Rabbit Fooled the Whale and the Elephant," by Sara Cone Bryant from *Stories to Tell to Children*, George G. Harrap & Co. Ltd., 1911. Used by permission of Chambers Publishers, Edinburgh, Scotland.

Adaptation of "The Tinker and the Ghost" from *Three Golden Oranges and Other Spanish Folk Tales* by Ralph Steele Boggs and Mary Gould Davis. Copyright © 1936 by David McKay Co., Inc. Copyright renewed 1964 by Ralph Steele Boggs and Perley B. Davis. Reprinted by permission of David McKay Co., a division of Random House, Inc.

Adaptation of "Monkey Business" by Ellen C. Babbitt from *Jakata Tales: Animal Stories*, copyright 1912, renewed 1940. Used by permission of Prentice-Hall, Inc., Englewood Cliffs, N.J.

Adaptation of "Why a Rabbitt Lives on the Moon" by Florence Sakade from *Japanese Children's Favorite Stories*. Charles E. Tuttle Co., Inc. 1958.

Adaptation of "The Cow on the Roof" by Thomas Gwynn Jones from *Welsh Folklore and Folk-Custom*. London: Methuen & Co. Copyright 1930, 1979 The estate of T. Gwynn Jones and Arthur ap Gwynn.

Adaptation of "Fair, Brown and Trembling" from *Celtic Fairy Tales*, collected by Joseph Jacobs. New York: Dover Publications, Inc. Used with permission.

Foreword

◆

Imagine flying around the world on a magic carpet and stopping to hear a story in each land you come to. This is what we feel we have been doing as we wrote and illustrated The Bedtime Story for The Kingston Whig-Standard. As the daily column was syndicated and picked up by other newspapers across the country, we flew a little farther and a little faster to bring our collection home, but what fun we have had!

There is probably no better way for parents to open their children's hearts to other cultures than by reading them fascinating tales from distant times and places. Stories of mystery, fun, pranks, ghosts, dragons and talking animals delight children of all ages, especially when shared in the warmth and stillness of bedtime. The special bond they form between the reader and the listener travels through time as well as the tales themselves.

This book is our treasure chest. In it are the gems of our collection. We hope they will charm, amuse and enrich you as much as they did us.

Amy Friedman and Jillian Hulme Gilliland

The Thieving Dragon

A Tale From Central Europe

◆

ONCE UPON A TIME, a gypsy and a shepherd were friends. The
gypsy visited the shepherd on the hillside and together they watched
the sheep graze. But one night the shepherd said to the gypsy,
"My friend, something is wrong. These last weeks, I have lost two
sheep each night. I have fallen asleep just before dawn, and that,
I am afraid, is when the thieving dragon comes and takes my sheep.
I am becoming poorer and poorer."

For a while the gypsy was quiet as he thought. He seemed to remember that long ago his father had told him tales of a thieving dragon. At last he said to his friend, "I will help you, friend. Tomorrow night I will come to your house. Tell your wife to prepare supper and to provide a good round cheese. After supper I will tend your sheep and I will catch the thieving dragon for you."

The next day the gypsy cut a branch from a willow tree. This he whittled down to a slender rod, and then back at his camp he searched until he found a heavy iron bar.

That night the gypsy went to the shepherd's house where the friends enjoyed a pleasant meal. As the sun set and the moon began to rise, the gypsy stood, and taking his slender wooden rod and his heavy iron bar and the round cheese which the shepherd's wife had given him, he strode off to the lonely hillside.

He sat upon the hill as the shepherd had night after night, and listened to the bleating of the sheep. He built a fire and listened to the crackling of the twigs. He looked up at the sky and watched the stars gleam. Long into the night the gypsy listened to the quiet munching of the animals and watched the fire and the stars. In this way he stayed awake through the night.

Suddenly, towards dawn, an enormous shape appeared on the hillside. The gypsy saw in the light of the fire that it was the fierce, thieving dragon.

"What is it that you want?" called the gypsy.

"I want two sheep for my breakfast," roared the ferocious dragon. The fire from his breath singed the whiskers on the gypsy's chin.

"These are not my sheep," called the gypsy, rubbing his warm face. "They belong to my friend the shepherd, and you have already stolen your share of his flock."

The dragon roared. "I shall take as many sheep as I wish. No one is strong enough to keep them from me."

"We'll see about that," called the gypsy, getting to his feet. "I am stronger than even a dragon, though I do not eat two sheep for breakfast every day."

"Ha!" roared the dragon. "Prove your strength and never again will I steal your friend the shepherd's sheep."

The gypsy stepped forward and showed the dragon his two sticks.

"See here, I have two sticks. Let us see which of us can throw his stick highest into the air." He held out his left hand and gave the dragon the iron bar. "You first," said the gypsy.

The dragon seized the iron bar and flung it high into the air. Up and up it went, and it climbed higher and higher, until at last it began its descent and fell to the ground with a thud.

The gypsy smiled. "My turn," he said. Holding the willow rod as if it weighed heavily, he whirled it around and twirled and whirled again. "Now look," the gypsy cried, and he pointed high into the sky. "Look up, look up!" As the dragon stared upwards the willow rod dropped down behind the gypsy's back. "You see," said the gypsy, "I have flung my stick so high it will never come down."

The dragon still stared up into the sky and waited, but nothing came down. "Now," said the gypsy, "do you believe that I am stronger than you are?"

The dragon roared. "Ha! You think that one test can prove your strength?"

"Then we shall have another contest," said the gypsy. "If I win this one, will you believe me?"

"Very well," the dragon said. "One more contest."

The gypsy picked up the round cheese that the shepherd's wife had given him.

"See this stone?" asked the gypsy. "I am so strong that I can crush it like a piece of clay." And he took the cheese in both hands and began to squeeze. He twisted and turned it and he grunted and he groaned and he squeezed. As the dragon watched, the cheese began to sweat watery milk from its skin until at last it crumbled into hundreds of pieces.

The dragon hissed flame.

Then the gypsy picked up a stone the size of the cheese and handed it to the dragon. "Here. Here's one for you," said he. The dragon took the stone between his two front paws and squeezed and squeezed with all his strength. Nothing at all happened to the stone.

The dragon threw the stone to the ground. "You win!" he said, shaking with fear. "You are stronger than I. Do not harm me," he begged. "I have an old mother who lives in a cave on the far side of this hill, and it is she who makes me steal sheep."

"You are lying," said the gypsy.

"Come, I shall take you to her."

"You may carry me upon your back," the gypsy said, "but don't forget how strong I am. I could kill you with one blow if I wished." The gypsy climbed up on the dragon's scaly back and he rode to the cave on the far side of the hill.

"Who's there?" cried the dragon's old mother, hearing footsteps approaching the cave.

"Someone much stronger than I," cried the dragon sadly. He told his mother of the gypsy's feats of strength.

The old mother sighed. "I once knew a gypsy who was just that strong," she told her son. "So I know that if this gypsy is as strong as you say, he is indeed stronger than you. I suppose I shall have to do without my sheep for breakfast."

For a moment the gypsy felt sad for the poor old dragon, but then he looked inside the cave and saw that she had saved dozens of sheep.

"But, you have enough to eat, Mother Dragon," said the gypsy.

"Yes," she said with a wink, "I do, gypsy. I only wished my son to learn the limits of his own strength."

"And so he has," said the gypsy.

"Tell me, gypsy," said the dragon, "Where did you get your strength from?"

"From my father, Mother Dragon. I shall give him your regards."

And with that the gypsy turned and left the cave and went back to his friend the shepherd.

"Your flock is safe," he said.

The shepherd was so grateful that he gave his friend a leg of mutton. The gypsy took it home and shared it with his parents, his wife and his children, changing their usually simple fare into a glorious feast, fit for fire-breathing dragons and fitter still for the gypsies who could outsmart them.

◆

The Magic Brocade

A Chinese Tale

◆

Part One

ONCE UPON A TIME, long, long ago, a mother lived with her three sons in southern China. She was a widow, and very poor, and she did her best to support her family by weaving magnificent, rich fabrics woven with designs of silver, gold and silk. The widow's brocades were so marvelous that they were known throughout the countryside. She wove birds and flowers and other animals into her cloth, and she was so talented that the creatures on her fabrics seemed to be alive. Some said her birds and flowers and animals were even more beautiful than real ones.

One day the widow went into the village to sell her beautiful brocades. In no time at all she had sold all her cloth, and so she strolled along, browsing through other market stalls.

Suddenly a beautiful picture caught her eye. There in the painting she saw an exquisite white house surrounded by enormous fields and long walkways leading to a garden that burst with fruits and flowers. In the background she saw smaller buildings. Great, glorious trees bloomed and dazzling plumed birds flew through the leaves of those trees.

The widow fell in love with the picture. She had to have it, and reaching into her purse she pulled out her coins and bought it. When she got home she showed the painting to her three sons, and they too were amazed by its beauty.

"Wouldn't it be grand to live in such a place," sighed the widow.

The two elder sons laughed and shook their heads. "Dear, dear mother," said the eldest son, "what idle dreams you have."

And the second son, still shaking his head, said, "Perhaps in the next world, dear mother, but not in this one."

But the third son put his arm around his mother's shoulders and said gently, "Why don't you weave a copy of this picture into your brocade? That will be nearly as good as living in it."

This idea made the mother very happy, and right away she went to the market and bought all the coloured yarn she would need to weave a copy of the painting into her brocade. Then she set up her loom and began.

Day and night, week after week, month after month, the widow sat at her loom weaving her silks. Her back began to ache and her eyes grew sore, but she would not stop. She worked late into the night, and sometimes all night long. She did nothing else but weave her brocade.

One day her sons came to her. The eldest grumbled angrily, "Mother, you weave all day and night, but you never go to market anymore to sell."

"Yes!" agreed the second son, angry too. "And we have to chop wood to earn money for the rice you eat. We're tired of all this hard work."

The youngest son was not angry. He put his arm around his mother's shoulder, trying to comfort her. Then he turned to his brothers and said, "Do not complain. I will look after everything for everyone."

From then on, every morning, the youngest son went up the mountain alone and chopped wood all day long. He chopped and chopped and chopped until he had enough wood to take care of the whole family.

Day after day, while her youngest son chopped wood, the widow wove. At night she burned pine branches so that she could see, and when the branches smoked, her eyes became bloodshot and sore. Still she worked.

A year passed. Tears from the widow's eyes dropped onto her picture, and so she wove the liquid into a crystal clear river and a little fish pond.

Another year passed. Now the tears from the widow's eyes turned to blood and dropped like jewels onto the cloth. The widow wove the droplets into a flaming red sun and brilliant red flowers. Hour after hour, day after day, month after month, she wove.

Finally, at the end of the third year, the brocade was complete. The widow stepped away from her work and smiled with pride. There it was: the exquisite house, the beautiful gardens, the exotic, flaming red flowers, the dazzling plumed birds. Sheep and cattle grazed contentedly in the vast, glistening green fields.

But suddenly, a great west wind howled through the house. The wind caught the brocade, whipped it into its arms and sped through the door. It flew up the hill, carrying the brocade along. The widow frantically chased after it, crying for her treasure, but she could only watch as the wind carried it high into the sky, far beyond her reach. She stood and watched in vain as the wind carried the brocade eastward, over the mountains. In the next moment it vanished from her sight.

The widow was heartbroken and fell into a deep faint. Her three sons carefully carried her into the house and laid her down upon her bed. They fed her ginger broth and tended her, and soon the widow awoke and looked up at her three sons. They saw the tears in her eyes.

"My son," she said to her eldest, "go to the east and find my brocade for me. It means more to me than life itself."

The boy nodded and quickly set off on his journey. He walked and walked and walked, and after a month he came to a mountain pass. There he saw an old, white-haired woman sitting in front of a small stone house. Beside the house stood trees with ripe, red fruit hanging from their branches. Standing beside the woman was a stone horse who looked for all the world as if he were about to eat the luscious fruit.

As the eldest son passed by, the old woman called to him, "Where are you going, young man?"

"East," he said to her. Then he told her the story of the wind's thievery.

"Ahh," said the old woman, "the brocade your mother wove has been taken by the fairies to Sun Mountain because it was so beautiful. They are going to copy it."

"Tell me," said the boy, more worried than ever, "how can I get it back?"

"That will be very difficult," said the old woman. "First you must knock out two of your front teeth and put them into the mouth of my stone horse. Then he will be able to move, and he will eat the red fruit hanging from this tree. When he has eaten ten pieces, you can mount him and he will take you to Sun Mountain."

The boy nodded. "But, before you reach Sun Mountain," the old woman went on, "you must pass through Flame Mountain which burns and burns and burns. You must not complain, for if you do you will be instantly burned to ashes. When you arrive at the other side, you must cross an icy sea. And if you shudder, even for a moment, you will immediately sink to the bottom of the sea."

After hearing what the old woman had told him about the flaming mountain and the icy sea, the eldest son stood and thought. He thought of the lashing waves of that icy sea, and he thought of the burning fires of the flaming mountain, and he turned as pale as a ghost.

The old woman looked at him and laughed. "You won't be able to stand the pain," she said. "I can see that now. Don't go. I will give you

a small box brimming with gold and you can take this to your mother and your brothers and you will live happily ever after in comfort."

The old woman stood up and moved into her house. She returned with a box of gold and this she gave to the eldest son who happily took it and turned homeward. But on his way, he began to think about all of the money he now had.

"This gold will allow me to live well, indeed," he said to himself. "But if I take it home I will have to share it with four people and it will not go far." Then and there he decided that he would not return to his family and he turned instead and headed towards the path that led to the big city.

The poor widow waited two long months for her eldest son's return. When he did not come back, she grew ill and decided at last that she must send her second son to fetch the brocade.

The second son rode off. When he reached the mountain pass he came upon the old woman outside her stone house beside the fruit trees and the great stone horse.

"Where are you going?" called the old woman to the second son.

"East," he said, and he too, told the story of the widow's brocade.

The old woman told the second son the same story she had told the eldest son. "You must knock out two of your front teeth," she said, "and these you will put into the mouth of the stone horse which will enable him to move. He will eat the red fruit hanging there. Then you can mount him and ride to Sun Mountain where the fairies have taken your mother's brocade."

The old woman went on to tell the second son about Flame Mountain. Again she explained, "You must not complain, for if you do, you will instantly be burned to ashes." And she told the second son about the icy sea, and gravely nodding she whispered, "If you give the slightest shudder, you will sink immediately to the bottom."

The second son, like his elder brother, grew pale as he thought about these trials. Again the old woman laughed, and again she offered a box of gold. Greatly relieved, the second son took the box of gold

and went on his way. Soon he decided that a box of gold would go much further if he kept it for himself. And so, like his brother, the second son turned towards the path that led to the big city.

After waiting and waiting and waiting for her second son to return, the old woman became very ill indeed. At last she was blind from weeping and still, neither son returned home.

The youngest son begged and begged his mother to let him go in search of the brocade. "I promise I shall bring it back to you, mother," he said. And at last, exhausted and despairing, the widow nodded and sent her third son on his way.

◆

Part Two

THE YOUNGEST SON took only two weeks to arrive at the mountain pass, for he travelled as swiftly as he could. When he arrived there he met the old woman in front of the stone house, and she told him exactly the things she had told his two elder brothers. But then she added, "Your brothers each went away with a box of gold, young man."

The boy steadfastly refused. "I shall not let these difficulties stop me," he told the old woman. "I promised my dear mother that I would bring her back the cloth she spent three years weaving. She is ill and sad, and I must bring her brocade back to her." And quickly he knocked two teeth out of his mouth and put these into the mouth of the handsome stone horse.

The stone horse came alive. He moved swiftly and gracefully towards the tall trees, and there he ate ten pieces of ripe, red fruit that hung from the branches. As soon as he had done this, he lifted his beautiful head, tossed his silvery mane, and he neighed. The youngest son mounted him and together they galloped off, towards the east.

After three days and three nights the young son came to Flame Mountain. On every side fires spit red-hot flames. For a moment the boy held the reigns back and stared at the wild sight, but then he spurred his horse and dashed up the fiery mountain, riding through the terrible heat without once uttering a word or a sound of complaint.

Once the youngest son and the horse reached the far side of the mountain, they came to a vast, vast sea. Great waves of ice crashed upon them as they made their way through frosty waters. They were cold and aching, and still the boy grasped the reigns and kept on his journey without ever once shuddering.

They reached the far shore of the icy sea and at once the youngest son saw Sun Mountain. Warm light flooded the sky, and everywhere fragrant flowers bloomed. And on top of Sun Mountain stood a marvelous palace. From the palace he could hear the sound of sweet laughter and singing.

Quickly he spurred his horse. It reared and galloped up the mountain to the door of the palace.

The boy climbed off his horse, walked through the palace door and into the great hall. There he saw a hundred beautiful fairies, each one sitting at a loom, weaving a copy of his mother's brocade.

The fairies were very surprised to see the boy standing there. For a moment no one said a word, and then one of the fairies stood up from her loom and came to him. "We shall finish our weaving tonight," she said, "and you may have your mother's brocade tomorrow. Will it please you to stay here the night?"

"Yes," said the youngest son, as he sat down to await his mother's treasure. If necessary he would wait forever.

The fairies brought him delicious fruit to refresh him after his difficult journey, and in a moment he was no longer the least bit tired.

When dusk fell the fairies hung an enormous pearl from the centre of the ceiling. The pearl shone so brightly it lit the entire room, and as the fairies went on weaving, the youngest son fell into a deep and wonderful sleep.

At last, in the middle of the night, one of the fairies finished her work. She sighed deeply as she looked at it, for her brocade was not nearly so beautiful as the one the widow had woven. She ached to think that she must now part with the old woman's treasure. She stared and stared at it, and the longer she stared, the more she wished that she could live in that beautiful human world. So she sat down again, and placing the widow's brocade upon her loom, she embroidered a picture of herself inside of it.

Just before daylight the youngest son woke from his deep sleep. He looked around and saw that the fairies had all disappeared. They had left his mother's exquisite brocade sitting beneath the shining pearl.

The boy could not wait for daybreak. He clasped the brocade to his chest, and mounting his brave, beautiful horse, he galloped off into the waning moonlight.

Again he and his horse came to the sea, and again the boy held tightly to the reigns, bent low and clamped his mouth tightly shut. Together he and his horse dived into the frigid waters. The horse's mane flowed and the boy held his breath, and neither of them so much as shuddered as they passed through the deep, icy sea.

On the far shore again the youngest son and the horse came to the flaming mountain. The boy clasped the reigns, spurred his brave horse and again they sped through wild flames. And once again neither horse nor boy uttered a word of complaint as together they passed through Flame Mountain and came out on the far side of it.

They came to the mountain pass where the old woman sat beside her stone house. "I see you have returned," said the old woman.

"Yes, old woman." He dismounted and when he did, the woman stood up and took the teeth from the horse's mouth. These she put back into the boy's mouth. In an instant the horse turned once again to stone.

"Wait here," the woman said to the youngest son and she went into her house. Soon she returned with a pair of deerskin shoes. "Take these," she said, "for they will help you to get home."

The boy put on the deerskin shoes and when he did he could suddenly move as if he had the wings of an angel. In a moment he was back at his mother's house in the room where she lay upon her bed, still very ill.

"Mother," he cried, and at that he unrolled her brocade. The cloth gleamed so brightly that the widow gasped. She blinked her eyes and discovered that her sight had returned. In a moment she was cured of her illness, and she rose from the bed and went to her son and thanked him for returning to her. And she thanked him for bringing back her beautiful brocade.

Together they lifted the cloth and took it outside to look at it in the sunlight. As they unrolled it, a strange breeze sprang up. It was a breeze so fragrant that it seemed to hold within it all the scents in the world. And the breeze blew upon the brocade, and it stretched it out, longer and longer and longer, and wider and wider and wider, until at last the brocade covered all the land in sight.

The silken threads began to tremble. Suddenly the picture sprang into life. The dazzling red flowers waved in a soft wind that stirred. Golden plumed birds darted in and out of the beautiful trees, and the animals breathed and bent their legs and rose and began to graze upon the glistening grass. The grand white house stood atop the hillside. It was all exactly as the widow had woven the scene. All but one thing.

Now, in the very centre, beside the crystal clear fish pond, stood a beautiful girl dressed all in red. It was the fairy who had embroidered herself into the brocade.

The kind widow, thrilled with her good fortune, went out to see all of her poor neighbours and invited each of them to come and live with her on her new land. She invited everyone to share the abundance of her rich, ripe fields and to share in the fruits and flowers of her magnificent garden.

And it probably will not surprise you to learn that the youngest son and the fairy looked at each other and fell instantly in love. And they married and lived together very happily for many, many years.

Then one day, many years later, two beggars came slowly down the road. They were the widow's two elder sons, and everyone could see clearly from their appearance that they had long, long ago wasted all the gold they once had.

The two beggars were astonished when they saw the magnificent white house and the lush green fields, and the dazzling garden and the exquisite birds, and the peaceful animals. They decided to stop and ask for something from the owner. But when they looked across the vast green fields, they suddenly recognized the people who were happily picnicking by the stream. They realized at once that two of the people were their very own mother and brother, and there was a beautiful lady with them who must be their brother's wife.

They watched for awhile and then, blushing with shame, they quickly picked up their walking sticks and crept silently away.

The Tiger, The Brahman and the Jackal

A Tale Told in India

◆

ONCE UPON A TIME, a tiger was prowling through the woods when suddenly – *Whump!* – a cage fell from a tree and the tiger was caught in a trap.

For hours and hours he tried to wedge himself through the narrow bars. He turned this way and that. He rolled around. When he discovered that he couldn't fit through, no matter which way he turned, he pawed at the bars and he shook them. At last he began to sob with grief and with rage, for he realized that nothing would work. He could not free himself.

The tiger had just lain down to weep over his plight when by chance along came a poor Brahman.

The tiger stood up at once and gleefully cried out, "Oh pious one, please, help me to get out of this cage!"

The Brahman stopped and calmly looked at the tiger. (Remember, the tiger was safely behind bars.) "No, my friend," said the Brahman. "For if I free you, you will no doubt eat me."

"No! I won't! On my honour. On the honour of my mother and father and all my brothers and sisters, I promise I won't eat you," the tiger cried. "On the contrary," he insisted, "I will always be grateful to you. I will be so grateful that I will, forever and ever, be your slave."

The tiger wept and wept, and the tiger made more and more promises. Then he said, "Oh kind, good sir, I have been here for hours, and soon I will die in this cage." And again the tiger began to sob and to tear at his fur.

The tiger's tears broke the poor Brahman's heart, and at last he could stand to see the tiger's pain no longer. He walked to the cage and opened the door.

The tiger leaped from the cage and grabbed the Brahman. "Ahh, what a fool you were," the tiger licked his lips. "What will prevent me from eating you now? I am starving after all the time I spent in that cage."

"But Tiger," the poor Brahman cried, "you promised me."

"Ah, but what is to force me to keep my promises?" asked the hungry tiger.

"Your good word," said the Brahman.

The tiger laughed and laughed.

"Then," said the Brahman, "promise me one thing."

"One thing then," the tiger said impatiently, for his stomach had begun to growl and he was eager to get on with his meal.

"I will go through the woods and ask the first three things I meet what they think of your promise. If they say that you have been unfair, you will free me. If they say you have been fair, I am yours."

The tiger was so hungry he could barely think, and he was tired of talking over the matter. So at last he agreed to the Brahman's deal. "All right, on with it, then," said the tiger. "Ask three things. And then return to tell me what you've heard."

The Brahman walked until he came upon a huge, old tree. "What do you think of this?" the Brahman asked the tree. "The tiger swore he would not eat me if I freed him from his cage. He wept and wept, so I freed him, and now he plans to eat me. Do you think that is fair?"

"You speak of fairness," the tree coldly answered, "and yet I stand here giving shade and shelter to all who pass by and they give me nothing in return. They tear my branches off to feed their cattle. They ignore my kindnesses. And do I whimper and complain? No, I do not. Stop whimpering now. Act like a man!"

The Brahman felt sad and hurt and he walked on, deeper into the woods. At last he saw a buffalo turning a well-wheel. "Good Buffalo," he said, "what do you think of the tiger's plan to eat me after I have saved his life and freed him from a cage?"

"Fool!" the buffalo spat. "You are a fool if you expect gratitude from anyone or anything. Look at me. I gave them milk to drink and they fed me cottonseed and oil-cake. And now that I am dry and have no more milk to offer, they yoke me here to work and feed me garbage!"

The Brahman felt sadder still at that. He looked down at the road. "Road, tell me. What do you think of the tiger's decision to eat me after I saved him from his trap?"

"My dear, dear sir," said the road, "you are foolish if you expect kindness for your kindness. Here I lie still and let everyone, rich and poor, fat and thin, good and bad, walk across me and ride their loads over me. Yet all, rich and poor, great and small, trample on me as they pass. What do they give me in return? They give me ashes from their pipes and husks from their grain and mud from their sandals!"

At this the Brahman felt sadder still for he realized that this was the end. He would have to let the tiger eat him, for no one he asked thought that the tiger's decision was unjust. And so he turned and began to walk back as slowly as he could.

On his way he met a jackal.

"Hey Mr. Brahman," called the jackal as he saw the sorrowful man passing by. "What's wrong with you? You look as unhappy as a fish out of water or a bird without wings."

The Brahman told the jackal his tale. The jackal scratched his head as he listened, and finally he said, "How confusing. Could you please tell me everything again? I got mixed up in your telling."

And so the Brahman told the whole story over again.

But once again the jackal shook his head and said, "I am so sorry, but I still do not understand. You tell me, and I listen to your tale, but I find I am still completely baffled. Perhaps if you take me to where this all happened, I will be able to make a better judgement about this matter."

The Brahman led the jackal to the cage. There the tiger stood waiting, his mouth watering and his stomach growling; he was sharpening his claws and teeth, readying himself for a magnificent meal. When he saw the Brahman he cried out, "Ah, there you are at last. You've been away for quite a long time!"

"Yes," said the Brahman sadly.

"Now then," said the tiger, "let us begin our meal."

"*Our* meal," thought the sad Brahman. His knees shook and his palms sweated, for he was terribly afraid.

"Please sir," said the Brahman, "if you will give me five more minutes so that I might explain the situation to the jackal here. He is somewhat slow-witted and I promised I would tell him what happened here."

The tiger nodded impatiently. "On with it then, hurry up." And once again the Brahman began to recite the whole tale, filling in all the details and making his story as long as possible.

"Oh my poor, poor brain!" cried the jackal. He scratched his head again and wrung his hands together. "I am sorry, but I cannot understand. Perhaps if you showed me how it all began. Let's see now . . . you say you were in the cage when the tiger came walking by?"

"Bah," cried the tiger, "you are a fool. *I* was the one in the cage!"

"Of course," cried the jackal, "*I* was in the cage." He began to tremble and to shake as if he were terribly afraid. "No, no, *I* wasn't in the cage. Dear me, I am still confused. Let me see now . . . the tiger was in the Brahman, you say, and along came the cage?"

"No you fool!" cried the tiger.

"Let's see then," said the jackal, "along came the cage to free the Brahman, and I was in the cage. No. No. Oh never mind, you must begin your dinner for I will never understand this tale."

The tiger was by now furious. "Yes, you will understand," ordered the tiger. "I will make you understand!" he roared. "Look here, I am the tiger."

"So you are," said the jackal. "And that is the Brahman," he said, pointing at the unhappy Brahman.

"Yes," said the Brahman, "that I am."

"And that is the cage."

"Yes, yes," said the tiger. "And I was in the cage. Understand?"

"Yes, no . . . oh my," cried the jackal, "I'm just not sure."

"What is wrong with you?" cried the tiger angrily.

"Just one thing," said the jackal, once more scratching his head. "How did you get into the cage?"

"In the usual way," growled the tiger.

"Dear me, my head is spinning again. Don't be angry with me, kind tiger, but what is the usual way?"

And at that the tiger lost all patience and jumped into the cage. "This way, you fool!" he roared. "Now, do you understand?"

"Perfectly," grinned the jackal. He quickly shut and locked the door. "And if you will permit me to say so, I think we shall leave matters as they were in the beginning."

And at that the tiger began once more to weep and wail. The Brahman bowed to the jackal. "Thank you, good sir for your generosity."

The jackal grinned. "My generosity?" he asked. "I simply hoped to understand. And now I do."

And the Brahman and the jackal went their separate ways.

Heart'N'Soul

A Tale From the Southern United States

◆

SOME OF YOU may have been standing in the village or along the roadside or at the river's edge on a day, not so long ago, when a young girl and her father passed by, leading their donkey. You may have heard the father call the donkey by her name. "Heart'N'Soul, y'all hurry up there now." Or you may have heard the young girl chide her. "Stop lagging, Heart'N'Soul, or you're gonna bother the creepers with your heavy hoofs."

Father and Daughter and their donkey, Heart'N'Soul, walked along, as you may know. They descended the Blue Ridge Mountains and moved into the valley. They walked on, crossing the rolling hills. On and on they went, all the way on foot to the river. They walked on, following the river's path across the countryside, then walked some more. The river was the James, and they were headed for Virginia's coast, the seaside and a ship that would sail them away to another land. They trudged through the thick brush, up and down the green hills. The sky was as blue as the bluebirds that sat upon the branches of the paradise trees. Some folks called those trees the Trees of Heaven, and so they seemed that day, at least for a while.

"We're gettin' closer," Father said to Daughter as he brushed her hair out of her eyes. She smiled up at him and they walked on.

The morning sun, rising fast, promised another sizzler; that's what Father called those long, August days. It was a southern summer day. Barn cats slithered, slow as they could, through thick cornfields. Mosquitoes buzzed and moaned. Spiders burrowed down deep into that red Virginia soil, seeking cool water. The river water, hot and still as the wind, seemed that day, not to flow at all. And still Father and Daughter walked leading their donkey, Heart'N'Soul.

At last, they reached a village where they passed a group of villagers sitting outside on a white, columned verandah. "H'lo there," called Father. Daughter waved and Heart'N'Soul brayed once, then looked up at Daughter and apologized for speaking out of turn. You may have been out on that porch sipping a nice, cool lemonade and watching this strange procession. You may have noticed that Father was old, with a withered face and worker's hands and sandals that were shedding their skin.

And you may have seen the men in their rockers, speaking so low that you wouldn't hear. "Just look at that, will ya?" one of the men said to his friends. "That poor old man walkin' like that while he could ride upon the donkey's back."

On Father and Daughter walked, and if you were sitting on that porch in that village by the James, you might just have seen what happened next. "Father," said Daughter, "you're getting old. Why don't you climb up on Heart'N'Soul's back and have a ride?"

"You heard them talkin', did ya darlin'?" asked Father.

"Yes, Father, I did." And Heart'N'Soul nodded, for she too, had heard. And so, without another moment's thought, the old man climbed up onto Heart'N'Soul's back and on they travelled, following the river's curve.

After a while, they passed a whitewashed church that stood just by the riverbank. "Will you look at that," you might have heard one of the church women whisper, in a whisper as loud as late winter wind. "That old man riding while his poor young thing walks in those threadbare shoes...why, it's a shame."

On past the church went Father, Daughter and Heart'N'Soul. Then just a bit farther on, Father looked down at his poor little daughter. He saw tiny, crystal beads of sweat gathering beneath her brow. "Sweet Daughter," he said, "why don't you climb up here with me?"

"You heard those women," said Daughter. And once more Heart'N' Soul nodded, and Father stopped her in her tracks, and up climbed Daughter, onto the donkey's back, and she sat just in front of Father.

"Now that's just fine," said Father. He gently kicked Heart'N'Soul's side, and once more they were on their way.

Now pretty soon, as luck would have it, they came to a bend in the river. They took the turn and happened upon a party of young folks in a field. The sun was high by then. If you were there you know just how hot and still that August day was, and just how lazy the young folks were feeling. If you were there you might have felt a little lazy yourself, and you might have wondered at this travelling band. And you might have said, just like the haughty boy in the swimming trunks said, loud enough so everyone could hear, "Will you just look at that." And you too, might have turned to look and you too, might have seen the sweating donkey carrying Father and Daughter down that dusty road. You might have felt like Father and Daughter, tired and hot, but dreaming of the scent of salty ocean air and cool, windy beaches.

"Now can you imagine treatin' an animal that way," the boy went on. You might have heard him if you were there in that field.

"Poor donkey," said one of the girls dressed in a soft summer dress.

"Imagine puttin' all that weight on a tired animal's back," said another, as she took a swig of ice cold rootbeer.

On walked Father, Daughter and Heart'N'Soul, but you can imagine what happened next.

"Father..." Daughter began.

"Yes," Father said, reading her mind. And they both looked down and saw how bony Heart'N'Soul's back was, and how sore her hoofs were.

And off they climbed, touching down once more onto the road. As soon as they did, the red dust rose and tickled their noses. They sneezed. Heart'N'Soul sneezed. You might have heard them if you were there, for the sound travelled far on that hot, windless day.

Heart'N'Soul looked down at the ground and Father saw how sad she seemed. And Daughter saw too.

"Perhaps," said Father, and Daughter nodded before he'd said another word. Then Father and Daughter together, reached out and lifted Heart'N'Soul into the air, balancing her upon their tired shoulders, and on they walked that way, carrying Heart'N'Soul. Everyone they passed shook their heads.

"What has gotten into their minds?" people whispered, very softly. "What kind of fool carries a donkey like that?"

No one ever found out if Father and Daughter reached the oceanside. But if you had been there, you might have told them that they ought not to listen to everyone's opinion all the time; that they ought to listen to their Heart'N'Soul, who knew them so well.

◆

The Dancing Stars

An Iroquois Legend From Canada

◆

Of all the stories there are about stars,
few are as lovely as this one.
Star gazers everywhere have noticed the same
patterns of stars in the same places in the heavens,
season after season.
Different stories about those same stars
have been told in every corner of the world.
This story was told in Canada,
around warm crackling fires, near tall straight trees,
under clear night skies.

LONG AGO, WHEN the earth and sky were new, seven sisters lived in a village. The sisters loved to dance. Every day they danced together in the forest, and wherever one sister went, the others followed. Every evening the sisters returned to the longhouse to rest, but by morning they were ready to dance again.

One evening, as the sun began to set, the sisters heard in the distance a glorious song. The song seemed to be calling to them, and in a moment they forgot about their suppers and they forgot about their home. For a moment, they stood still and listened, and then, without speaking a word, they danced off towards the source of the song.

They danced through open spaces and into the forest. On they danced as the sun dipped towards the horizon. The stars began to gleam and the sky grew darker, but still the sisters danced towards the sound. Then suddenly, their feet seemed lighter. When they looked down they saw that everything they had ever known was far below them. They were dancing up into the sky.

They danced on, higher and higher, moving towards the beautiful sound, and the song grew louder and louder, and more and more beautiful, and more and more mysterious. Below them the longhouses and the trees and their friends and families seemed to grow smaller and smaller. And finally, the song became a sweet, gentle voice.

I came to the sky
for a hunter pursued me.
And now I am lost in the sky.
Come, my sisters,
come here to me in the sky.
And I will watch over you.

Then the sisters saw who was singing the song. It was a great black bear. Her tail glistened, for it was strewn with stars, and around her neck she wore a shimmering necklace of stars. Her nose and her toes twinkled with stars and around her belly hung a belt of shining stars.

The sisters danced closer and closer, and the bear went on singing. On and on she sang, as the sisters went on dancing. They danced for hours, and the great black bear sang and her toes and nose and tail and neck and belly glistened.

After many, many hours the sisters looked up and saw how very dark it was, and how far away they had travelled, and they could not remember the way home.

The moon smiled and winked and watched as the sisters went on dancing. "My children," she said, "this is your home now. The stars and I love the way you dance, and we wish you to live here with us."

The sisters leaped and twirled and whirled and swayed and twisted and tapped and toed. To their amazement, they did not grow tired. They twirled faster, they whirled faster, and each time they twirled another star twinkled and grew.

Then suddenly, the smallest sister heard another voice. She heard it over the sound of the song and over the tapping of her sisters' feet. And she knew it was her mother's voice. Her mother was calling to her.

The smallest sister began to run towards her mother's voice. "Come back!" cried the six dancing sisters, but the little girl was racing now. "Come back, little sister," called the dancing girls once again, and they watched as the child ran with a bright star trailing her.

Together the youngest sister and the star descended from the sky. Down, down, down they sped, past clouds and past the eagle's nest, and past the tallest branches of the trees. Down, down, down.

At last the smallest sister saw her mother and she raced faster still. Finally, she landed on the ground. But as her feet touched the earth she vanished. And there, in her place was simply a hole.

The mother looked down at the hole, and she began to weep. Then she looked into the sky and she saw her other daughters dancing still.

"Stay in the sky," she called to warn them. "Stay there and dance with the great black bear or you will crash to earth."

The sisters heard their mother's warning over the sound of the great black bear's song, and they nodded their heads and waved and smiled as the stars behind them twinkled more brightly. "Yes, mother," they called, "we will stay in the sky."

Down below, the mother sat and wept. Her tears splashed one by one into the earth where her daughter had vanished. But soon, to her joy, a small green shoot sprang up from the hole, drawing strength from the tears that watered it. Quickly it grew, higher and higher. The youngest child was reaching up to her sisters. Higher the shoot grew, until at last, it reached the stars.

Today the tall, tall tree still stands; the tallest tree in the whole world. And when you look up at the sky, you will see seven dancing sisters. You may even hear the song of the great black bear who sings a lullaby for all her children.

The Lizard's Sorrow

A Tale From Southeast Asia

ONCE UPON A TIME, there was a very rich man whose house was filled with treasures. One of his favourite pastimes was playing a game he had invented. It went something like this:

The first man would name one of his belongings. "I have a stable filled with fifty cows," he might say, to which the challenger might answer, "And so do I," but only if he did own fifty cows. Then the first man might say, "I sleep in a bed that is made of the finest teak, encrusted with diamonds," and if the challenger slept on a simple reed mat, he lost the game. It was a rich man's game, and this man was rich indeed. He loved to beat all those who challenged him and boast about his wealth as well.

One day a stranger appeared at the rich man's door. The gatekeeper could see with one glance that the stranger was a beggar. His clothes were tattered and his straw sandals were frayed. He carried a bag made of rough cotton tied together by four frayed ends. The stranger's face was pale and thin and he looked as if he had not eaten for days.

"Please," the stranger gently asked the gatekeeper, "may I come in? I wish to play your master's game with him."

The gatekeeper stared in wonder, but the stranger seemed so dignified and gracious that he could not say no, and so he opened wide the gates. Then he went to tell his master of the visitor's request.

The rich man was intrigued that a beggar wished to play his game and so he ordered his servant to bid the man enter.

Looking haggard and weary, the stranger walked into the elegant room. The rich man offered him a chair covered with fine brocade, and he called to his servants to bring hot tea in priceless, porcelain bowls. "Now my friend, is it true that you wish to play a game of riches with me?" asked the rich man.

"Yes," said the stranger, sipping his tea and sitting at ease in the chair. "That is what I wish to do, if you will allow me the pleasure."

"Yes, of course," said the rich man. "But may I ask who you are and where you have come from?"

The stranger smiled. "You need not know this," he said gently. "I came from afar to play your game. That is all. However, if you will allow me to tell you, I do have two conditions before we play."

"Tell me what they are," said the rich man, for by now he was curious indeed.

The visitor leaned back in his beautiful chair. "A game is fun only if someone wins and someone loses. May I suggest that if I win I take everything in your possession; all of your belongings. And if you win," and at this the stranger paused and smiled, "if you win, you will have everything that belongs to me. And sir, I should tell you that I am one of the most fortunate men in the entire world."

The rich man laughed.

"One more thing," said the visitor. "If you win, I shall stay here until the end of my life and serve you."

The rich man stared in silence for a moment, thinking that this stranger must be mad. At last he answered, "I'll agree. But you said you had two conditions. Tell me, what is the second?"

The stranger looked out of the window and gazed for some time at the lush rice paddies and then up at the glittering blue sky. At last he spoke in his quiet, gentle voice. "My second condition is only that you will give me, a mere visitor, the pleasure of asking the first question."

"Agreed," said the rich man, for he was certain that he owned everything imaginable, and surely he owned far more than anything this poor stranger could possess.

"Are you sure?" asked the visitor.

The rich man cringed. He was worried by the stranger's doubt, and he knew now there was no way out of the game. "Yes, I agree," he repeated irritably, "I've told you I agree. Now what is it you have that I do not own?"

The stranger put down his teacup and carefully, slowly, he opened his travelling bag. From it he pulled an empty half of an old, chipped coconut shell.

The rich man stared. "A coconut shell!" he cried. "And it's chipped!" The servants stared, not knowing whether the rich man was shattered or amused at the sight of this sad-looking object.

"This is the cup I use to drink from on my wanderings," said the visitor.

"Certainly I have such an object," exclaimed the rich man. He sent his servants scurrying off to search every nook and corner of the house for a chipped coconut shell.

Alas, no one could find such an object in the rich man's house. The servants had coconut shells in their kitchen, but these were clean and unbroken, for they lived in the house of a wealthy man who bought only the finest of things.

"Only a beggar would drink from such a cup," cried the rich man. "I do not have such a horrid thing."

Again the visitor smiled calmly. "Sir," said he, "this coconut shell is many years old, and it is the only object that I own besides these tattered clothes and my worn sandals and my carrying bag. But I value this cup more than you do all the treasures that you own, for it allows me to quench my thirst as I wander through the land. I am certain I love my cup more than you do all your precious china."

The rich man could not say a word. The stranger went on. "And now sir, I own all your treasures and belongings for you agreed to my conditions, and I have won the game."

The stranger moved into the rich man's house and at once began to give away all the rich man's possessions: his land and his herds, his furniture and his china, his clothing and his carpets. He gave these to the poor and needy in the land. And then one day, he took up his bag, placed his old coconut shell inside of it and wandered off once more. No one in all the land ever saw him again.

No one knows exactly what became of the rich man. Some say that he died of grief on the day he lost the game. But most say that he was transformed into a tiny lizard such as the lizards that scurry about inside many peoples' houses. These lizards are three inches long with webbed feet and short, round heads. With sad faces, they run about all day and night, upside down on the ceiling, along the walls, across the floors, and all day and all night they cry out "Tsst, tsst, tsst," as if they were wailing, "Oh, if only I had known … If only I had known … if only, if only…."

These are the sorriest of all earth's creatures. They possess nothing and they scurry away into small dark places whenever strangers approach. So, if you should suddenly come upon a lizard hiding – say, in a porcelain tea cup or an old coconut shell – take pity on it. Perhaps you have found a once rich and very foolish man.

◆

Orpheus and Eurydice

A Greek Myth Retold by Peter and Amy Friedman

◆

*In ancient times the Greeks believed there were many gods
who ruled the earth and planets,
and they believed those gods lived on Mount Olympus.*

*Apollo, glorious god of the sun, and Calliope,
beloved muse of poetry, gave birth to a son there.
They named him Orpheus. As a birth gift, Apollo
gave the child a lyre, and though Orpheus had many
heroic adventures, he is best remembered
for the beautiful music he played on the instrument.
When Orpheus died, his heartbroken father
placed the lyre among the stars.
It shines there still.*

Part One

LONG, LONG AGO, when the gods ruled Mount Olympus, a little boy named Orpheus could be heard plucking the strings of his lyre. This was no ordinary boy, for he was the son of the great god Apollo. And this was no ordinary lyre, for Apollo himself had given it to Orpheus on the day he was born.

As Orpheus grew, so did his skill with the instrument. He learned to play the lyre with such nimble fingers, that soon he was known throughout the land as a musician beyond compare. His songs were magical, graceful and joyous.

When Orpheus played, savage beasts lay down in the tall grass and became the gentlest of creatures. His music was so enchanting, that hearing it, people felt peaceful and happy. Flowers bloomed at the sound of those strings, and stars glowed more brightly as the notes climbed to the heavens. Even the rocks became soft when Orpheus played.

Orpheus loved his lyre more than he loved anything – until the day he happened upon a beautiful young girl who was playing in the fields with her friends. At the sight of her, Orpheus fell instantly in love. Her name was Eurydice. As Orpheus watched her romp and run, he played his lyre more beautifully than ever. Eurydice turned to look, and she too, fell at once in love. Within days, Orpheus and Eurydice announced that they would wed.

The wedding of Eurydice and Orpheus was most wonderful. Every woman, man, beast and god came to a field of golden flowers and blossoming trees for the celebration, and there, altogether, gods and mortals and beasts rejoiced. Throughout the day they feasted, danced and sang and toasted the happy couple.

One day, not long after the wedding, Eurydice went off to the fields with her friends to romp and run. As they played, a shepherd sitting upon a nearby hill watched. Wanting a closer look, he got up and walked slowly towards the girls. And when he saw Eurydice, he gasped with admiration at her grace and lively spirit. Moving closer still, he caught her eye and began to flirt with her. Eurydice, alarmed by the stranger, quickly fled. She dashed through the fields, past trees, into the deepest grass, back towards the house she shared with her beloved husband. But as she ran, a hissing serpent rose from the deep grass and bit her ankle. A moment later, Eurydice was dead.

When Orpheus heard the news, he was distraught. He wept and cried to the gods and to his friends. And then, knowing that he could not live without Eurydice, he embarked upon a long and dangerous journey to the Underworld to find her.

The journey to the Underworld is terrible and difficult. As Orpheus started on his descent, people pleaded with him not to go. "This is impossible, dear Orpheus," some cried. "The cruelest of creatures protect the gates of Hades. No man can pass them safely."

"Orpheus," others begged, "please stay. You will never survive the dangers that lurk beyond the Underworld gates."

But Orpheus would not listen. He thought only of Eurydice. And so the people cried more loudly still. "Orpheus, please don't go. In the Underworld even your glorious music will not protect you."

Orpheus could not be stopped. He went on, moving towards the Underworld, all the while playing sad songs upon his lyre.

After many days of treacherous travel, Orpheus came upon the Styx, a roiling, rolling river. The only way to cross the Styx was by the ferry that was captained by a hard-hearted, cruel ferryman who had never carried a living soul across that dangerous waterway. Orpheus began to play his lyre with all his heart, more beautifully than he had ever played, and the ferryman's heart softened. Tears came to his eyes. In an instant, he beckoned Orpheus aboard and ferried him across the Styx.

As they rode, Orpheus could hear the ominous growls of Cerberus, the three-headed dog who guarded the gates of Hades. When the ferry landed, Orpheus stepped off and looked into this creature's angry eyes. At once Orpheus took up his lyre and began to play more loudly, more lyrically, more gracefully and lovingly than before. At once Cerberus, like the savage beasts on earth, turned gentle and fell fast asleep.

Orpheus quickly moved through the gates and in a moment he stood before Hades, god of the Underworld. Hades' eyes were dark as midnight and deeper than the deepest well. In a voice so loud the sound pierced Orpheus' very heart, Hades cried, "Begone! No living man is welcome here."

But Orpheus would not be daunted. "I come here not to plunder or wreak havoc on this land. I come for love alone," said Orpheus. "I love Eurydice. I must take her back with me to the land of the living."

Hades stared coldly at Orpheus. His eyes seemed to grow darker still, and he did not say a word.

Orpheus went on, his voice pleading. "You know that Eurydice and I must eventually return here. Please give us our time together on earth. Give us only that."

Still Hades stared. But the dark spirits of the Underworld had awakened. The Furies, daughters of darkness, screamed and howled. Tisiphone, Avenger of Blood, said, "Hades, we can murder him," while the implacable Alecto crossed her arms and shook her head. "Never, never, never..." And then, Megaera, ever jealous, cried, "He'll not have his beloved. How can he love anyone but me?"

Orpheus looked at each of them in turn.

At that moment, Persephone stepped from the darkness and stood beside Hades, her husband. Orpheus, without saying another word, began to play upon his lyre.

Though Orpheus played his lover's lament from deep within his being, he dared not hope his melody would move dead hearts and souls. The music spilled around him, and soon the aching chords began to waft throughout the Underworld, reaching its dark and secret crevices.

As if by magic, everyone's hearts began to soften, and soon even the Furies were weeping tender tears. Soon too, Persephone's heart began to ache as Orpheus' did. She looked into her husband's eyes and said, "You must grant his request."

Even Hades submitted to the lure of Orpheus' harp. "You may have your wife," he said, "but only upon one condition. You will travel back to earth and Eurydice will follow you. But you must not look back at her until you reach the light of day. If you look, you will lose her."

♦

Part Two

ORPHEUS WAS THE happiest of men, and Eurydice the happiest of women as she followed behind Orpheus on their difficult journey. They walked and walked and walked, for the Underworld is a distant land, and the journey is longer than any other. Orpheus stared straight ahead and strode with great determination. All the time he thought only of how he loved Eurydice. He thought of her beautiful face, her gentle voice, her graceful, kind nature, her love for him and he thought of her walking behind him. He listened for her footsteps, but he heard only silence. Still, he walked on.

Moving through a cavern filled with slippery rocks, spiders and slithery creatures, Orpheus hesitated. Was Eurydice behind him? He dared not look back. He walked on, through mossy caverns, deep, dank caves, across the foaming Styx. He longed to ask the ferryman, "Is Eurydice there?" No. He would not ask. He simply rode across the river, thinking of her.

On he went, thinking of how he loved his wife. He thought of how joyful they would be when once more they were arm in arm. He remembered her face. He remembered how lovely she had looked when he first saw her. He nearly tripped as he walked a narrow pathway bounded by cavernous drops. He gasped, listened, but heard nothing behind him.

On he trudged until at last he saw ahead of him the glowing light of day. He ran towards the light with his heart pounding so hard he could not hear another sound. He ran and ran, out of the last of the dark caverns and caves, through grey, heavy mist. And just when he emerged into the light, he thought: Is Eurydice still on my heels? Will she too, move now into the light of day? Will we once again play in our beloved fields?

Without thinking, he turned.

Yes, Eurydice was there walking quickly, but still within the dark shadows of the Underworld. Seeing his beloved, Orpheus reached for her. And Eurydice reached for him.

Too late. Orpheus had disobeyed Hades' command. The moment he turned, Eurydice began to fall. Down, down, down she tumbled, down through the last cavern, down and down and down still deeper towards the world they had almost escaped. Orpheus reached out his arms once more, but he touched only air. Eurydice was gone.

Orpheus ran back towards the Underworld, back into the mossy, damp caverns, back to the darkest of places. For an instant he saw her in the distance, falling, falling, falling, and then he lost sight of her altogether.

He ran faster still, down and down and down, with beating heart. And now he came upon the ferryman again. Orpheus began to play his lyre, but this time even the sweetest song did not touch the ferryman's heart.

"I've lost Eurydice again!" Orpheus cried.

But the ferryman just shook his head and said gruffly, "No living passengers."

Orpheus played his lyre as he had never played. All those above, on earth, living in light, could hear his song. Every man and god and beast in the light of the world began to weep. But the ferryman would not be moved.

At last Orpheus saw he had no chance. With tears in his eyes and a pain that pierced deeper than any lance, he trudged back towards the light of day.

Now Orpheus wept and wailed all day, every day, and when he walked through the forests playing his lyre, the beasts, hearing the sound, lay down and cried with him. Even flowers wilted, shedding dewy tears.

Day after day after day Orpheus walked alone. Unable to speak, the only thing he could do was to play his sad songs. Everywhere the pain of Orpheus' broken heart pierced the hearts of those who heard the sound. Orpheus' grief lay like a veil upon the land, the seas and the heavens.

At last the beasts gathered together. "He cannot live this way," cried the tiger. "We must find some way to ease his pain."

And so the beasts made a plan together. It was the only plan that could put an end to Orpheus' grief at last.

As Orpheus walked through the fields, still playing upon his lyre, the lions signalled all the other beasts. Out they came from behind every weeping bush and wailing tree and wilting flower. They ran towards Orpheus and attacked. In a moment Orpheus was dead.

The woeful music stopped. Down, down, down went Orpheus, into the darkness of the Underworld. And this time he was welcomed, for he too, was a dead soul. The ferryman, without a word, carried him across the roiling Styx. This time Cerberus did not hesitate to open wide the gates and welcome Orpheus to the land of the dead. Then Hades bade him enter.

At once, upon arriving, Orpheus ran to his beloved Eurydice and they embraced. And ever since that day, Orpheus and Eurydice have wandered arm in arm through the dark fields of the Underworld, filled with joy at their reunion, always and forever in love.

◆

Talk

An African Ashanti Tale by Harold Courlander and George Herzog

ONCE, NOT FAR from the city of Accra on the Gulf of Guinea, a country man went out to his garden to dig up some yams to take to market. While he was digging, one of the yams said to him, "Well, at last you're here. You never weeded me, but now you come around with your digging stick. Go away and leave me alone!"

The farmer turned around and looked at his cow in amazement. The cow was chewing her cud and looking at him.

"Did you say something?" he asked.

The cow kept on chewing and said nothing, but the man's dog spoke up. "It wasn't the cow who spoke to you," the dog said. "It was the yam. The yam says leave him alone."

The man became angry, because his dog had never talked before, and he didn't like his tone besides. So he took his knife and cut a branch from a palm tree to whip his dog. Just then the palm tree said, "Put that branch down!"

The man was getting very upset about the way things were going, and he started to throw the palm branch away, but the palm branch said, "Man, put me down softly!"

He put the branch down gently on a stone, and the stone said, "Hey, take that thing off me!"

This was enough, and the frightened farmer started to run for his village. On the way he met a fisherman going the other way with a fish trap on his head.

"What's the hurry?" the fisherman asked.

"My yam said, 'Leave me alone!' Then the dog said, 'Listen to what the yam says!' When I went to whip the dog with a palm branch the tree said, 'Put that branch down!' Then the palm branch said, 'Do it softly!' Then the stone said, 'Take that thing off me!'"

"Is that all?" the man with the fish trap asked. "Is that so frightening?"

"Well," the man's fish trap said, "did he take it off the stone?"

"Wah!" the fisherman shouted. He threw the fish trap on the ground and began to run with the farmer, and on the trail they met a weaver with a bundle of cloth on his head.

"Where are you going in such a rush?" he asked them.

"My yam said, 'Leave me alone!'" the farmer said. "The dog said, 'Listen to what the yam says!' The tree said, 'Put that branch down!' The branch said, 'Do it softly!' And the stone said, 'Take that thing off me!'"

"And then," the fisherman continued, "the fish trap said, 'Did he take it off?'"

"That's nothing to get excited about," the weaver said. "No reason at all."

"Oh, yes it is," his bundle of cloth said. "If it happened to you you'd run too!"

"Wah!" the weaver shouted. He threw his bundle on the trail and started running with the other men.

They came panting to the ford in the river and found a man bathing. "Are you chasing a gazelle?" he asked them.

The first man said breathlessly, "My yam talked at me, and it said, 'Leave me alone!' And my dog said, 'Listen to your yam!' And when I cut myself a branch the tree said, 'Put that branch down!' And the branch said, 'Do it softly!' And the stone said, 'Take that thing off me!'"

The fisherman panted, "And my trap said, 'Did he?'"

The weaver wheezed, "And my bundle of cloth said, 'You'd run too!'"

"Is that why you're running?" the man in the river asked.

"Well, wouldn't you run if you were in their position?" the river said.

The man jumped out of the water and began to run with the others. They ran down the main street of the village to the house of the chief. The chief's servant brought his stool out, and he came and sat on it to listen to their complaints. The men began to recite their troubles.

"I went out to my garden to dig yams," the farmer said, waving his arms. "Then everything began to talk! My yam said, 'Leave me alone!'

My dog said, 'Pay attention to your yam!' The tree said, 'Put that branch down!' The branch said, 'Do it softly!' And the stone said, 'Take it off me!' "

"And my fish trap said, 'Well, did he take it off?' " the fisherman said.

"And my cloth said, 'You'd run too!' " the weaver said.

"And the river said the same," the bather said hoarsely, his eyes bulging.

The chief listened to them patiently, but he couldn't refrain from scowling. "Now this is really a wild story," he said at last. "You'd better all go back to your work before I punish you for disturbing the peace."

So the men went away, and the chief shook his head and mumbled to himself, "Nonsense like that upsets the community."

"Fantastic, isn't it?" his stool said. "Imagine, a talking yam!"

◆

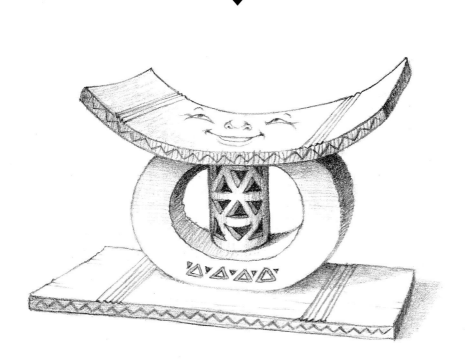

The Three Hares

A Fable Told in Turkey

ONCE UPON A TIME, three baby hares lived with their father and mother in a very deep and narrow hole in the ground. When they were still very young, their father said to them, "Little ones, you have been given large ears. Use them well and pay close attention to my words, for what I have to say to you now is very important."

The three hares pricked up their ears and leaned in close to listen carefully.

"You are now grown. Today is the end of your first month of life, and tomorrow your second month of life begins. Tonight or tomorrow your mother will give birth to your brothers and sisters. We cannot all stay here together for our hole is very narrow. Therefore, you must each go out and dig your own run and make your own nest. Make it deep and narrow. That is our custom, my children."

The three hares looked at each other, and then they looked back at their father to hear more about the custom of the hares.

"When your mother and I were one month old we each left our homes and not much later we met each other. Remember, my little ones, try to settle somewhere nearby so that we will remain close to each other. And remember too, never trust a crafty fox."

When Father Hare had finished speaking, the three young hares hopped over to their mother and said goodbye. Then they hopped over to their father and said goodbye to him. And then they jumped up, out of the hole and went their separate ways.

The first hare said to himself, said he: "I am not going to dig a hole like my father's hole. That dark, dark den made me feel ill, and I have had enough of that sort of life. Besides, the weather up here is lovely. I shall build a little cottage in the most beautiful place I can find. It shall be near the woods and the meadows, and I shall go out whenever I wish and I shall look out my window and enjoy the beautiful countryside."

So the first little hare collected moss and sticks and stones and leaves and brush, and with these he built himself a lovely little house. Then he went inside and settled down in a corner and looked out at the countryside. In a little while he began to feel hungry, so he hopped outside to look for food. And while he was scouting through the meadows, a fox came upon him and said: "Hare, hare, little downy hare, stop and talk to me. Let us be friends, little hare. Don't run from me. I won't hurt you."

But the little hare was not stupid. "Oh, cunning-eyed fox," he said, "I know you would like to catch me and eat me, but you shall not!"

And with that he leaped into the air and bounded through the long meadow grass and into his little cottage.

A few minutes later the fox was at the cottage, and moments later he was pulling down the house, munching the sticks and straw and all the other goodies that the hare had used to build his little house. And in another moment—scrunch, munch, crunch—the fox had eaten the first little hare.

The second young hare was not much different from her brother. "I have grown tired of that dark, dark house my father built," she said to herself. "I shall make a nest here in the roots of this beautiful tree."

So the second little hare carried moss and twigs and straw and scraps of everything that she could find to the roots of the tree, and then she crept inside her nest and sat. When she began to feel hungry she went outside to find some food, and while she was grazing in the beautiful meadow, along came the wily fox.

"Hare, hare, little hare," called the fox, "oh downy hare, my friend. Don't run from me. Let us talk and visit with each other. I mean you no harm."

But the little hare cried out, "Oh ho, fox, I know you are no friend. My father warned me about you. You would eat me if you could, but you'll never catch me!" And with that the second little hare leaped into the air and bounded through the meadow and into her nest.

When the fox saw the second hare's nest, he began to laugh. "Silly hare," he called, "now you shall see that I can eat you up in one single gulp!" And in just a few minutes the fox had torn apart the second nest of sticks and straws and moss and he had eaten the second hare, scrunch, munch, crunch.

The third little hare, meanwhile, hopped through the woods and said to himself: "I shall dig a hole somewhere near my father's den, and then I shall get inside and make myself comfortable in my new home."

So he set to work very quickly and he dug for a day and a night. By the second day he had made a winding run that was deep and long, and narrow. When it was finished, he climbed inside and hid. As soon as he was hungry, he came out again, and he hopped to the beautiful meadow. There, sure enough, he met up with the fox, and once again the crafty fox called out, "Oh, downy little hare, come talk to me. I would never hurt a hair on your head."

"Cunning fox," said the third little hare, "sharp-nosed fox, I know your tricks. Do you think the other animals didn't tell me that only yesterday you gobbled up my sister and the day before that you gobbled up my brother? You'll never catch me, wily fox."

And off he ran, leaping into the air and bounding across the grass and down, down, down he went, into his narrow, twisting, deep, dark lair. The fox trotted quickly after him, but try as he might he could not get into the hole. He waited a while. He panted and he waited, and he waited some more. But the third hare was too smart to come out of his lair while he could hear the fox breathing above him.

At last the fox gave up and walked off. And that is how the third little hare proved himself to be more clever than his brother and his sister. He lived close to his parents and had children of his own. And most of them, the ones with large ears, lived safely from all foxes, dogs and hunters forever afterwards!

◆

Mr. Lazybones

A Tale Told in Laos

◆

ONCE UPON A TIME a man called Mr. Lazybones lived beneath a
wild fig tree. All day and all night he lay beneath the wild fig and waited
for the fruits to fall into his mouth.

People everywhere gossiped about Mr. Lazybones, mocking him and
calling him names. "He's never worked a day in his life," they sneered.
"He'll never amount to anything," they whispered. "He never plants or
hunts," they snapped. "If those figs didn't drop, he would starve."

Sometimes people threw rocks at him and called him names and teased him mercilessly. But Mr. Lazybones was so lazy that he didn't bother to answer them back. He simply sat still with his mouth opened wide, awaiting the moment for the fruit to fall and land upon his tongue.

One day a great wind began to blow and as the figs dropped, the wind swept them up and tossed them through the air. They landed in a nearby stream and floated downstream, bobbing and twirling in the flow of the current.

The king's niece, whiling away an hour or two, sat on the riverbank. When she saw the figs float by, she reached down, picked one up and ate it.

"How delicious!" she exclaimed. "This is the most wonderful fruit I've ever eaten." Then and there she vowed that she would find the man who grew the figs and marry him.

The king promised his niece he would help her find the owner of the figs. He ordered all the fig growers from every corner of the land to bring a sample of their fruit to court.

From near and far the fig growers came. They brought their fruits to the palace and set them on a long table spread with white silk.

The king's niece tasted each fig one by one. "Uncle, all of these are very tasty," said the pretty princess, "but none is so delicious as the fig I ate beside the stream. Surely someone has not brought his wares."

"Ladies and gentlemen," called the king, "is there any fig grower in all this land who has not appeared before my niece?"

The people began to laugh. They told the king that only one fig grower in all the land had not appeared at the palace, and that was Mr. Lazybones who was too lazy to journey to court.

When the princess heard this news she decided to visit Mr. Lazybones herself. And so she set off.

She found him lying half-asleep beneath his tree. She reached up and plucked a fig and tasted it. At once she knew she had found the man she would marry – the grower of the most delicious figs in the kingdom.

The king was upset upon hearing this news. "Niece, are you certain that you want to marry such a lazy man?" he asked.

"Yes, Uncle, I am certain."

"Marry him then," said the king, "but if you do, you will lose your inheritance. Furthermore, you and he may never live beneath this palace roof."

Mr. Lazybones and the princess did marry and for a time they lived happily together beneath the precious fig tree. They ate and ate the delicious figs to their hearts' content.

But then one day something terrible happened. The fig tree stopped bearing fruit. The king's niece was so used to her diet of figs, and had become so lazy from lying under the tree, that she fell seriously ill. Mr. Lazybones wept, for he dearly loved his wife. Never had anyone been so kind and good to him.

To keep his wife alive, Mr. Lazybones knew he would have to do the one thing he hated most in life. He would have to work.

So at once he set to growing new fig trees. He ploughed and planted and watered and pruned under the hot sun, and never once did he complain. Soon, due to his hard work, the new trees grew large and fruitful, and the land became lush. With figs to eat, Mr. Lazybones' wife was restored to health.

When the king learned of the work that Mr. Lazybones had done and of the love he had shown for the princess, he returned the inheritance and invited the couple to live in the palace with him. Mr. Lazybones and his wife lived comfortably and happily in the palace, and once again Mr. Lazybones did not have to work. Often, sitting upon his chair, he would think. Then one day he said to his wife, "When I was poor and lazy people called me Mr. Lazybones and teased me. But now that I am rich and lazy, they call me Prince and praise my name."

And thinking of this, the couple laughed quietly to themselves, reached for two more figs and chuckled at the foolishness of folk.

◆

Anansi
Plays With Fire

A Caribbean Tale

♦

In the Caribbean everyone knows Anansi, half man and half spider.
Everyone knows Anansi plays tricks on everyone,
and everyone gets angry or upset or tired of him.
Everyone knows no matter what,
Anansi is always everywhere and that he likes music and food
and dancing and he likes all the things everyone likes.
Anansi is no loner. Anansi is a troublemaker. Everyone knows that.

ANANSI WATCHED FROM a distance when the great rustle and bustle began in preparation for Tiger's wedding feast. This feast was going to be special. Everyone knew that. All the creatures prepared, except one. One was not invited. That one was Anansi.

Tiger was tired of Anansi, tired of his mean tricks. So Anansi said to himself, "I must do something about this. Oh to think of all the eating and the dancing I will miss." And if Anansi had not been so angry at Tiger, Anansi might have felt very sad.

Anansi walked to Tiger's house and looked inside and saw Tiger hustling and bustling in preparation for his wedding.

"Mmmm," Anansi inhaled the scent of sweet curry and coconut. "Mmmm hmmm hmmm." Then Anansi said, "Morning to you, Bredda Tiger. I see you are cooking some fine, fine food."

Tiger growled at Anansi and went on cooking.

"Heard you are marrying a fine, fine girl tomorrow, Bredda Tiger," said Anansi, ignoring Tiger's growl and his scowl.

"Grrrr," Tiger said. "Grrrr, grrrr, grrrr."

Anansi ignored that and said, "Heard you invited everyone. Heard every creature plans to come. Heard about everyone but me, your friend Anansi." And with that Anansi smiled his sweetest smile.

"Grrrrrrrrr," growled Tiger. Anansi's sweet smile couldn't fool Tiger. Not now. Tiger knew Anansi was a troublemaker. Everyone knew that.

Still, Anansi went on. "Never thought a friend would treat another friend this way. After all we been through together, Bredda Tiger. Thought you would ask Friend Anansi to your wedding."

Tiger couldn't stand it any longer, so he growled, "Get out of here you thief. You liar! You cheat! Get out of here before I pay you back for all the trouble you have brought to everyone. This is one day you will never spoil!"

This was too much for Anansi. He stopped smiling. "Ha, Bredda Tiger," he said. "You'll see. I'll find a way to spoil your wedding day good and rotten. I'll give you plenty trouble, you'll see. I'll put a spell on you." And with that Anansi ran away.

Tiger began to worry. People said Anansi was a magician and could cast a spell. "Maybe I should talk to my bride," he said to himself. "Maybe we should invite Anansi to our wedding, even though he lied and cheated and tricked me so many times." And thinking that, he went off to see his bride.

When he got to Anita's house he saw her face and heard her voice, and he thought only of their wedding plans. He forgot all about curses and spells. He forget all about Anansi.

Only Anansi did not forget. "I'll fix that mean Tiger," he said. All of his legs shook with rage. Then he began to wend his way back towards Tiger's house, but he did not go straight there. No, Anansi never goes anywhere straight. He went all around until he came to Tiger's house and then he stopped and looked, and seeing no one was about, he ran to the forest to search for a cowitch creeper.

Now everyone knows the cowitch creeper is a vine that crawls and creeps up trunks and branches. Everyone knows that those velvety pods that look so nice and soft and sweet and make you want to touch them, are not so very sweet after all. Everyone wants to touch them, and everyone knows if you do your skin will burn and itch until you'll want to jump into a river to cool. And still, you will have to scratch until your skin is raw. And then still, you'll keep on scratching.

Anansi covered his bare hands with leaves and then he cut the creepers and holding them far from his body, he carried them back to Tiger's house. And there, on Tiger's table, he saw Tiger's wedding clothes. Mean Anansi took those pods and rubbed them all over all those fine, fine clothes. And when he finished that, he ran away again.

Early next day Tiger put on his fine wedding clothes and soon Dog and Horse and Cat and Monkey and Bird and Frog and Snake and Turtle and Lion and Bee came to help him prepare for the wedding. Everyone came except Anansi.

But in a minute Tiger began to itch and itch until he couldn't stand it anymore! He tore off his clothes and looked at them, and all the other animals looked too, and then they saw, upon the floor, the cowitch creeper pods, and they knew what Anansi had done.

The animals whispered and talked altogether. They must get Anansi this time, they said. They had to pay him back for all his cruel tricks, they said to each other. "Yes, we must," they all agreed. And they talked and talked until at last they came up with a plan.

Bee flew off to fetch Anansi. She did not have to fly very far for Anansi was nearby, hopping around, waiting to hear the news of how his trick had worked.

Bee landed beside Anansi. "Anansiiii," she buzzed, "come! There's plenty food left at the wedding feast." As everyone knows, Anansi has the biggest appetite of anyone, and he could not resist. Off he went with Bee.

Now all the creatures gathered round Anansi until there was nowhere for Anansi to turn. And Tiger roared: "Now we have you, Anansi, and we'll show you!"

Anansi grew pale and every single one of his legs trembled with fright. Monkey and Horse and Cat ran to the trees and returned with heaps of cowitch creeper. Then they lay these on the ground and made a bed of them. And then Snake hissed, "Now, ssssss, we'll put you on this bed of cowitch, ssssss, and we'll roll you around and around, ssssss."

"No!" cried Anansi, "I'm your old friend, Bredda Tiger. It was a joke, that's all!"

But Tiger roared, "And now it's time for our little joke," and all the animals threw Anansi onto the cowitch and rolled him around and around, and Anansi burned and itched like grass on fire.

Then all at once Anansi knew what he must do. "Bredda Tiger," he cried, "look out there. I see the Queen! She's coming down the road."

"A trick," hissed Snake. "Don't listen to Anansi, friends."

"It's not a trick," cried Anansi. "The papers announced her arrival, but you were all too busy with the wedding plans to pay any attention. Now she's here. The Queen! You must look!"

Everyone doubted Anansi, but then, everyone knows how that goes. You never know. You never know when a liar might be telling you the truth. And then the animals heard a sound. It was the wind whistling in the trees. But Anansi said, "Listen, that's the sound of the people cheering. Better hurry or you won't see the Queen." And all the animals believed him and they turned and ran to see the Queen who was not there, and Anansi ran the other way to jump into the cool river.

And that is how the troublemaker, Anansi was tricked that one time, but got away just the same. Everyone knows that!

The Flying Ship

A Russian Tale

◆

When two French brothers, Joseph and Jacques Montgolfier,
began their experiments, they probably never dreamed
they were on the verge of an invention
that would eventually lead to the entire science
of flight and aviation. In 1872,
they began filling paper and fabric bags with hot air.
A year later, they had made the first hot air balloon.
It wasn't exactly a flying ship like the one in this story.
However, in the minds of those who watched
from the ground, the first humans to take to the air
must have been either magnificent heroes
or fools of the world!

Part One

ONCE UPON A TIME there lived an old man and an old woman and their three sons. The two eldest sons were very clever, but the third son was not so wise as his brothers. In fact, sometimes he was very foolish indeed. Some children are like that.

The old man and woman treated their two wise sons very well. The old woman cooked wonderful meals for her eldest sons, but she often forgot even to feed her young, foolish son. She washed and mended her eldest sons' clothing, but the youngest son wore tattered, dirty clothes, for the old woman ignored him. The old man called his youngest son the Fool of the World.

One day the Tsar of that country sent out messengers to every part of his land, even to the smallest villages, inviting people to the palace for a feast. The messengers told the people that the Tsar would give his daughter's hand in marriage to any man who could bring to the celebration a flying ship; a ship that could fly through the blue, blue skies the way most ships sail the high, blue seas.

"Here is our chance," said the two wise brothers. "Surely such wise men as we can find a flying ship."

"Yes," said the old man and woman. "You must set off immediately."

So the old woman packed a basket filled with soft, white bread and many different kinds of meat and she filled flasks with the finest vodka. She walked her two eldest sons to the end of the village road, and there she waved and waved until they were long out of sight.

And so the two wise brothers went happily off on their adventure, but no one knows what happened to them for no one ever heard from them again.

The Fool of the World stood by and watched as his brothers set off. "I'd like to go to the palace too," he told his parents. "And I too, would like to marry the Tsar's daughter."

"You're a fool," said the old woman. "What good would it do you to go?"

The old man shook his head. "If you set off into the woods you will meet with a bear who will eat you. Or the wolves will attack you and tear you to pieces before you even notice them," said the old man to his son.

But the Fool of the World was determined. "I want to go," he said. "I will go," he said. "I want to go. I will go. I want to go. I will go." He repeated and repeated, until at last his parents saw that there was nothing to be done to change his mind. Besides, they could no longer

stand the sound of his voice, so the old woman packed a paper sack with crusts of dry, black bread and a few pieces of stale meat. She filled his flask with water and saw him to the door of the hut, and as soon as he walked out the door she closed it behind him and turned back to her chores.

The Fool of the World set off happily with his paper bag in his hand, singing as he walked, for he was going to seek his fortune and to marry the Tsar's daughter. What could be better than that? He was sorry not to have soft, white bread or fresh meat, and he was sorry too, that he did not have any vodka, but after all he had water and something to eat, and the day was beautiful. And so he sang as he walked through the lush green forest, beneath the dazzling blue sky.

The Fool of the World had not gone very far when he passed an old, old man with a long, long beard and dark eyes hidden beneath bushy, white eyebrows.

"Good day, young fellow," said the old man.

"Good day, grandfather," said the Fool of the World.

"Where are you off to?" asked the old man.

"You mean to say you haven't heard?" cried the Fool of the World. "I am going to the palace of the Tsar for he has promised his daughter's hand in marriage to the man who can bring him a flying ship."

"Do you have a flying ship?" asked the old man.

"No," said the Fool of the World.

"Then what will you do?" asked the old man.

"Who knows?" said the Fool of the World.

"Then you won't mind sitting down and sharing a bit of your food?"

"I am ashamed to offer you the food I have," said the Fool of the World. "It is good enough for me, but it is hardly food fit for guests."

"Never mind," said the old man. "Anything would taste fine."

And so the Fool of the World opened his bag to offer his stale, black bread to the old man, but to his surprise he found inside fresh, white bread and many different kinds of meat. These he offered to the old man.

"You see," said the old man, "you too shall have your share of good things. And now," he said as he ate a piece of soft, white bread, "let us drink some vodka."

"I'm afraid I have only water," said the Fool of the World. But to his amazement, when he opened his flask he saw the finest vodka. And so the pair merrily ate and drank and when they had finished they sang a song or two.

Then the old man said, "Now, you go off into the forest. When you come to the first big tree you must stop there and strike it a blow with your small hatchet. Then, fall backwards on the ground and lie there until someone comes to wake you. When you wake you will see a ship ready to fly. Then you must climb inside and fly off to wherever you wish to fly, but be sure as you fly through the countryside to give a ride to everyone you meet on your way."

The Fool of the World thanked the old man and walked into the forest. He came upon a large tree, and as he had promised, he swung his hatchet around his head and struck a blow on the truck. Instantly he fell down and lay on the ground. He closed his eyes and went at once to sleep.

Some time passed, and then the Fool felt something tugging at him. When he opened his eyes, he saw no living thing. But there, where the large tree had stood, he saw a beautiful ship with silken sails and golden trim. It was the most beautiful ship he had ever seen. He jumped inside, and the moment that he grabbed the tiller, the ship took off into the air. The Fool of the World sailed off into the blue, blue sky in his magnificent flying ship.

On and on the Fool of the World sailed in his flying ship, steering a course over the road so that he would not lose his way to the Tsar's palace.

Suddenly he looked down and he saw below him a man lying on the road with his ear to the ground. "Good day, uncle," cried the Fool of the World, "what are you doing down there?"

"Good day, Flying Fellow," cried the man. "I am listening to everything that is happening in the world."

"Come ride with me," said the Fool, and the man happily agreed. The Fool swooped down and picked up the Listener and off they sailed through the skies together, singing songs.

After they had flown on for awhile the Fool looked down and saw a man walking along the road on one leg. His other leg was tied up to his ear, much to the Fool's surprise.

"Good day, uncle," cried the Fool, bringing his ship close to the ground. "Why are you walking on one foot?"

"Good day, Sky Man," said the hopping man. "I walk this way because if I untied the other foot I would step across the world in a single stride."

"Why walk at all when you could ride with us?" said the Fool. So, the Hopper happily climbed into the ship with the Fool and the Listener.

On and on they flew until they saw a man on the ground with a bow and arrow. He was aiming at something, but the men in the ship saw nothing. "Good day, uncle," cried the Fool swooping down to the ground. "What will you shoot at? I see no beasts about."

"Ah, Air Man, you see nothing, but everything is visible to me," said the Archer. "The invisible is my target."

"Come with us, then," said the Fool, "we're going to the Tsar's palace to feast," and so the Archer climbed aboard. Off flew the Fool and the Listener and the Hopper and the Archer through the skies.

Suddenly, they saw a man on the ground carrying an enormous sack filled with many, many loaves of bread. "Good day to you," cried the Fool to the man with the bread. "Where are you going down there?"

"Good day, Man of the Sky. I am going to get bread for my supper," cried the man with the many loaves.

"But you already have a sack full of bread," cried the Fool.

"Oh, this little bit! This is not enough for one mouthful."

"Then take a seat with us," cried the Fool, "and come to the Tsar's feast to eat, Gobbler."

And so the Gobbler climbed on board and they flew on, singing louder than ever before. On and on they flew and then they saw below them a man walking round and round a lake, looking for something.

"Good day, uncle," cried the Fool. "What is it you seek down there?"

"Good day, Cloud Man," cried the searching man. "I am looking for water to drink."

"But you are standing at the edge of a lake," said the Fool. "Take a drink of that."

"That!" spat the man at the lake. "That's but a drop. If I took one gulp it would be gone."

"Then come with us to the Tsar's feast," said the Fool, "and drink your fill there." The Drinker climbed aboard.

On they flew until they saw a man carrying wood on his shoulders. He was walking with his wood into the forest. "Good day, uncle," said the Fool. "Why are you taking that wood into the forest?" he asked the man.

"This wood is special, Sky Man," said the Woodman. "If I scatter these pieces, a whole army of soldiers will leap up from the ground."

"You must come with us to see the Tsar then," said the Fool, and the Woodman climbed aboard.

They rose higher and higher into the air and sang louder and louder. Suddenly they saw below them a man carrying a sackful of straw, and they zoomed down to speak to him. "Good health, uncle," cried the Fool to the man carrying straw. "What do you intend to do with that straw you carry?"

"Ah, Flying Man, this is special straw. If you scatter it on hot, hot days, the weather turns to frost and snow in an instant."

"Come with us to the Tsar's palace," said the Fool and the Strawman hopped onto the flying ship and joined the rest of the happy, singing crew.

They flew on and on, altogether now, singing and laughing and enjoying the beautiful skies, and then they came to the Tsar's palace. They cast anchor and floated down to the courtyard.

The Tsar heard their singing as they landed, and he looked out and saw the ship of his dreams sail to earth. "Ah," he thought. "The prince who has made a flying ship." He called to his servant and asked him to go out to discover what prince it was who guided the exquisite flying ship to earth while singing such beautiful songs.

But when the servant saw the Fool of the World and his companions who were sitting onboard the flying ship telling jokes to each other and laughing and enjoying the day, he stared. What was this? These were all simply peasants, men dressed in tattered clothing. These were no princes!

And so, without saying a word, the servant returned to the Tsar to tell him of the sad, sad news. The Tsar was not pleased to hear what the servant had learned, for he did not want his daughter to marry a simple peasant.

"What shall I do?" he thought, trying to figure out some way to get out of the bargain he had made. All the people in the country knew that the Tsar had promised his daughter's hand to any man who could bring him a flying ship.

"But a peasant!" worried the Tsar. "No, a peasant is not good enough for my only daughter." So he sat in his palace until at last he came up with a plan to save his daughter from marrying a peasant in a flying ship. The Tsar would set a task so difficult that the peasant would be unable to perform it. And when he failed, he would flee the palace, leaving the flying ship behind him.

Part Two

PLEASED WITH HIS plan, the Tsar sent his servant to tell the peasant what he must do. "Tell him he must fetch me some magical water of life and he must do this before we have finished eating our supper. If he can complete this task, he may have my daughter's hand."

As the Tsar spoke, Listener, the first of the Fool of the World's companions, heard and ran to tell the Fool.

The Fool stopped laughing and singing. "What on earth will I do?" he asked sadly. "I could not find the magical water of life if I had a lifetime to look, yet the Tsar wants it before he has finished his supper."

"Don't you worry about that," said Hopper, the Fool's second companion. Freeing the foot which had been tied to his head, he ran off, and faster than you can say, "water of life," he arrived at the water of life and poured some of the magical liquid into a bottle. And then, feeling a little weary, he thought, "I have plenty of time to return. I shall just sit and rest a bit." He sat down beside a windmill and went to sleep.

Back at the palace the royal supper was nearly finished. The men sat in the flying ship, but they no longer sang or told jokes. Quiet and restless, they waited for Hopper to return with the water of life. "Where can he be?" fretted The Fool of the World. "If Hopper does not return soon, I will not be able to marry the princess."

Listener put his ear to the ground. "What a joker," he cried. "Hopper has gone to sleep beside the windmill by the water of life. I can hear him snoring. I can hear the sound of the windmill turning. And I can hear a fly buzzing in the air around the windmill."

"I'll take care of that," said Archer, and picking up his bow and arrow he aimed at the fly. His arrow sailed across the land and through the air. As it pierced the fly, the creature cried out and woke Hopper who leaped from the ground. In less time than it takes to say "magic water," he was back at the flying ship. He gave the magic water of life to the Fool, and the Fool gave it to the servant who took it to the palace and offered it to the Tsar, saying, "Here is the magic water of life, just as you asked."

The Tsar had not left the supper table, and so The Fool of the World had performed the task just as the Tsar had asked.

"These are cunning fellows, these peasants," he cried. "I must set them another task to perform." He said to his servant, "Tell the peasant with the flying ship that he and his companions are to eat, at a single meal, forty roasted oxen and forty loaves of bread. That should fix him," laughed the Tsar.

The servant returned to the flying ship and told the peasants of the Tsar's command.

"Fine," said the Fool of the World. "Send along the food."

The servant sent to the flying ship forty roasted oxen and forty loaves of bread, and everyone sat down to eat. But before the rest could open their mouths, Gobbler had eaten every bit. "Hardly any food at all," said Gobbler, wiping his mouth with a napkin. "I could eat forty more oxen and still feel hungry."

When the servant saw that the food was gone, he hurried back to the palace.

"Well then!" cried the Tsar. "Tell the peasants that they must drink forty barrels of vodka and forty barrels of water too, and if they fail they will die by my sword!"

And so the servant sent to the men forty barrels of vodka and forty barrels of water, and in less than a moment, Drinker consumed every ounce. Then he leaned back and patted his stomach. "No trouble at all. If only I had a few more barrels, I might be less thirsty."

The servant again reported to the Tsar. "They have eaten all the oxen and the bread," he said, "and now they have finished every last drop of vodka and water."

The Tsar fumed. "What shall I do? I must get rid of this peasant." And he thought of yet another plan.

"Very well," he said to his servant. "Tell the fellow to prepare for the wedding. He must go and bathe in the palace bathhouse. But let the bathhouse be made so hot that any man who enters will burn himself to ashes the moment he sets foot inside."

The servant went to the bathhouse which was made of iron, and he made it so hot that no man who entered could live.

But Listener had overheard the Tsar, and he told the Fool of the World. "What shall I do now?" cried the Fool. "If I go to the bathhouse to prepare for my wedding, I will burn to ashes."

But Strawman patted the Fool of the World on the back and said, "Never you fear." He went to the bathhouse and scattered his straw at the entrance. It became so cold inside that when the Fool of the World entered to bathe himself, he began to shiver. He was so cold that he lay down on the stove and curled up and slept through the night. In the morning when the servants opened the door they found him sitting atop the stove and smiling.

The Tsar was furious. "Tell this fellow that if he is to marry my daughter he must show me that he can defend her," he cried. Of course, Listener heard and told the Fool who asked his friends, "How can I defend a princess?"

This time Woodman came to his rescue. At night while everyone slept, he scattered his sticks everywhere, and in the morning an army appeared, so enormous that no one could even count the number of soldiers. When the Tsar saw this, he was afraid. If this peasant had such an army, it might be best to test him no further. So, the Tsar took riches and fine clothes to the men on the flying ship, and he took them himself, instead of sending his servant. They were invited to the palace, and there, the Tsar gave the Fool of the World his daughter's hand in marriage.

The Fool of the World, dressed in those fine clothes, looked as handsome as any prince has ever looked. The princess fell in love with him at once, for she loved his generosity and his kindness and his cheerful nature and the way he sang. They were married and lived forever afterwards in great happiness.

It Could Always Be Worse

A Story From Central Europe

THERE ONCE WAS a poor man whose life was so miserable, he was at the end of his wits. It was clear he needed advice, and so he went to see his rabbi.

"Holy Rabbi," the poor man cried. "I'm in a bad way and things are getting worse all the time! We are so poor, so poor, that my wife and six children and my in-laws and I all live together in a tiny one-room hut. We are always in each others' way, our nerves are bad and we quarrel because we have so many troubles. Believe me, Rabbi, my home is terrible. I'd rather die than go on in this way."

The rabbi thought and thought about what the man had told him and at last he said, "Son, promise me that you will do as I tell you. If you do, I assure you, your situation will improve."

"I promise, Rabbi," said the poor man. "I'll do anything you say."

"Tell me then, son. What animals do you own?"

"I own a cow, a goat and a few chickens."

"Very well then," said the rabbi. "Go home and take all these animals into your home to live with you."

The poor man stared at the rabbi. He couldn't believe his ears, but he had promised. He went home and took all the animals into his house.

The next day the poor man returned to the rabbi. "Oh Rabbi, Rabbi, you have brought such misfortune upon me!" he cried. "I kept my promise. I went home and took all of my animals into my house. And now things are worse than ever. My house has become a barn! Rabbi, Rabbi, please help me. My life isn't worth living now."

"Son," the rabbi said calmly, "go home now and take the chickens outside. God will surely help you."

And so the poor man returned home and took the chickens outside, but very soon afterwards he came running again to the rabbi.

"Holy Rabbi," he cried, "please, you must save me. The goat is smashing everything inside my house. She breaks cups and saucers everywhere. I can't live this way, Rabbi. The goat has turned my life into a waking nightmare."

"Go home then, son," the rabbi said gently. "Take the goat outside now. God will help you."

And so the poor man went home and took the goat outside. But before long he came running back to the rabbi. "Oh Rabbi, Rabbi," the man cried, "what misery you have caused me. The cow turns my house into a stable. She stinks and moos all night long. How can you expect human beings to live peacefully side by side with an animal like that?"

"Of course," said the rabbi, "you are right. You must go straight home and take that cow out of your house."

The poor man returned to his house and took the cow outside.

The next day the man came running once more to the rabbi. But this time he was smiling happily.

"Oh Rabbi," he cried, "you have made my life sweet. With all the animals outside again our house is quiet, and so roomy, and so clean. Rabbi. You have saved my life!"

And with that, the wise rabbi smiled, and sent the happy man home to the peace and harmony of his little family and his spacious one-room hut.

How Brother Rabbit Fooled Whale and Elephant

An African Fable

◆

ONE COOL AUTUMN day, little Brother Rabbit was hopping along the sand – clippety, clappety, lippety, lappety – when he saw Whale and Elephant talking to each other at the edge of the sea. Little Brother Rabbit crouched down in the sand and raised his ears to hear what they were saying.

"Brother Elephant," said Whale in her deep, deep voice, "you are the biggest creature on the land, and I am the biggest creature in the sea. Together you and I could rule all the animals in this whole wide world. We could have everything our own way."

Elephant raised his mighty head and trumpeted, "Good, good, good. Oh yes, that would be fine by me. We must come up with a plan."

Little Brother Rabbit laughed to himself and thought, "They won't rule me. I have a plan of my own!" He ran away to the edge of the sand and found a nice strong rope. Then he picked up his drum and hid it in the bushes. And then – clippety, clappety, lippety, lappety – he hopped back to the water's edge.

There little Brother Rabbit met Whale.

"Oh please, Sister Whale," he said in his sweetest, most timid voice. "Won't you do me a great big favour? My cow is stuck in the mud a little distance from here and I can't get her out. You are so strong and so big and so kind. Please say you will help me with my problem."

Whale puffed up with pride, and so flattered was she that without a moment's hesitation, she looked at little Brother Rabbit and said, "Yes. Of course I'll help."

Little Brother Rabbit held up his long, strong rope. "Then I will tie this end of my long rope to you, and I will run down the beach and tie the other end to my cow. When my cow is tied fast, I will beat my drum. When you hear the sound, please, would you pull very hard? My cow, I'm afraid, is stuck very deep, so it will take all of your strength to move her."

"Ha!" said Whale, "A cow won't require a bit of my strength. I could pull her out if she were stuck up to her horns."

Rabbit smiled broadly and nodded his thanks. Then he tied the rope-end to Whale and ran off down the beach until he met up with Elephant.

"Oh please, Brother Elephant," Rabbit pleaded softly, bowing deeply to show his respect, "I need your help. Would such a big, strong elephant as you consider helping a poor little rabbit like me?"

Elephant looked down over his long, long trunk at Rabbit. "What is it you want?" he grunted.

"My cow is stuck deep in the mud just down the beach and I cannot rescue her. But you are so strong, and with your help –"

But before Rabbit could finish his flattery, Elephant snorted grandly, "Of course I'll help."

"Oh thank you!" said Rabbit. "I will tie one end of this rope to your trunk and I'll hop down the beach to my cow. As soon as I have tied her tightly I will beat my drum. Then you must pull very hard for my cow is stuck deep in the mud, and she is very heavy."

"No problem," said Elephant. "I could pull a dozen cows and still have strength to spare."

"Oh yes, I know," said little Brother Rabbit politely, "but be sure to begin by pulling gently, for I don't want to hurt her."

Rabbit tied the rope to Elephant's trunk and ran away into the bushes.

There he sat down and waited for a moment or two, laughing to himself. Then Rabbit began to beat his drum. *Tarum, tarum, tarum.*

When Whale heard the sound, she began to pull.

Elephant, hearing the drumming in the distance, began to pull at the same time. In no time at all, the rope was as tight as could be.

Elephant heaved. "My, this is a heavy, heavy cow," he said to himself. He dug his feet into the sand and gave another great tug.

Whale was amazed by the strength of the pull on the far end of the rope. "Dear me," she said. "That cow must be stuck deeper than Rabbit thought." And she pulled with all her might, and then she pulled harder still.

Down the beach, in the setting sun, Elephant found a tree and braced himself against its bark and tugged. With each tug he wrapped a bit of rope around his trunk and pulled again.

Whale began to slide towards land. She became so angry with the cow that she dived deep, deep, deeper into the water until she reached the bottom of the sea.

At the far end of the rope Elephant lost his footing and came slipping and sliding down the beach and, whoosh! He slipped right into the cold, wet surf. He cursed the cow and braced himself and pulled with all his might.

Whale came shooting up out of the sea, sputtering water. "Who, who is, who is pulling me?" she stuttered and spat.

"Who on earth has such strength?" Elephant bellowed.

Then at last they saw each other, and they saw that each of them held one end of the rope.

Elephant roared in a rage, "I'll teach you to pretend you are a cow!" and Whale spouted again and fumed, "I'll show you not to try to fool a whale!" And they began all over again to pull as hard as they could. But this time, stretched beyond its strength, the rope broke in two. Whale fell back into the sea in a great somersault, and Elephant fell onto his back on the hot, scratchy sand.

When Whale had righted herself and Elephant got to his feet, they were too ashamed to say a word to each other.

And that ended their friendship, and their bargain too. And little Brother Rabbit, still very much his own boss, sat in the bushes and laughed and laughed.

◆

The Tinker and the Ghost

A Tale Told in Spain

◆

*November 1 is All Saint's Day, and Hallowe'en
or All Hallow's Eve is celebrated the night before.
Hallowe'en started from the ancient belief
that as summer ended and the warmth of the sun faded,
all life was coming to an end. People
imagined that on this night, ghosts, witches
and restless spirits came back to haunt their old homes.
In those days, people lit bonfires to calm
the spirits and to strengthen the dying
flames of the sun.
With time beliefs change, but even now on Hallowe'en
jack o' lanterns light the way for any little spooks
who might be about to pay us a visit.*

Part One

LONG, LONG AGO, on a Spanish plain near the city of Toledo, a huge grey castle stood deserted for many years. It was deserted because it was haunted. No living soul lived inside the castle, but almost every night all year long, people in the village could hear a thin, sad voice moaning and groaning and weeping and wailing. And every year on All Hallows' Eve, a ghostly light would appear in the chimney. The light would flare against the dark sky, die, and flare again. This would continue all night long on that one dark eve when ghosts and goblins prowl.

The owner of the castle offered to pay a handsome sum to anyone who could rid the castle of its ghost. Brilliant doctors and brave adventurers and wise people came to the castle from near and far, all of them promising to exorcise the castle of its ghost. But always, the next morning when the villagers came to see what had happened, they would find the doctor or the wise person or the brave adventurer sitting lifeless before the cold hearth in the castle's great hall.

Then on the very last day of October, a brave and jolly tinker named Esteban came to this little village on the Spanish plain. Esteban sat in the marketplace mending the villagers' pots and pans, and after awhile he learned about the haunted castle from the gossipers in the town.

On All Hallows' Eve, they said, if he waited until nightfall, he would see the strange ghost appear like a flare in the chimney. And he might, they said, if he dared go near enough to the castle, hear the thin, sad voice that echoed through the dark, empty rooms.

"If I dare!" Esteban said with great scorn, for he was a very brave tinker. "You must know, good people, that I – Esteban – fear nothing. I fear no human being and I fear no ghosts. And I will gladly sleep in that castle tonight and keep the poor, sad spirit company for it sounds as if it is lonely."

The good people of the village looked with amazement at Esteban. Did he know that if he succeeded in ridding the castle of the ghost that the owner would give him a thousand gold pieces? Did he know he would be a rich man if he were brave enough to do this deed?

Esteban chuckled at that. No, he had not known, but if that was how things were, he would go that very night and do his best to rid the place of the thing that haunted it.

But, he added, he was a man who liked to have good food to eat and plenty to drink and he would want a fire to keep him warm and serve as a companion. So, he told the villagers that they must bring him a load of sticks to build a fire and a side of bacon and a flask of good wine and a dozen large, white eggs and a large frying pan. And, he said, with these provisions, he would be merrily on his way to the castle.

The good people of the village were happy to provide these things, and they gathered all he had requested, stowed it in a pack and saddled Esteban's donkey for the ride to the haunted castle.

As dusk fell Esteban mounted his donkey and set off. For a short while some of the villagers followed the brave tinker, but you may be sure they did not go far, for they were afraid of the castle at night. So, one by one the villagers returned home, leaving Esteban to travel on his own.

And so Esteban journeyed on up the hill through the dark, dark night. A chill wind whistled shrilly through the trees, and the air felt heavy, as if rain might fall at any moment. Still Esteban rode, feeling fine and fit, for you must remember he was a very brave and very jolly fellow.

Esteban reached the castle, unsaddled his donkey and set the animal to graze upon the grass outside the castle walls. Then he carried his food and sticks and frying pan and wine into the great, draughty hall.

Inside it was pitch dark. Esteban could hear bats beating their soft wings as they flew across the empty room. He felt their bodies whisk like feathers across his face. The air was musty, and he could hear the wind shrieking outside the castle walls.

In the room near the hearth, he took his pile of sticks from his pack, lit them, and in a moment golden red flames leaped up towards the chimney and began to warm the room.

Esteban leaned towards the fire and settled himself comfortably. And then, rubbing his hands together and holding them over the flames, he sighed, "Now there's just the thing to keep off both cold and fear."

Then Esteban reached into his pack and removed the bacon. This he carefully sliced and slipped into the pan which he set upon the fire. As the bacon fried, its aroma filled the room. Esteban inhaled deeply, enjoying the delicious smell and delighting in the sound of the crisp sizzle.

He had just lifted the flask full of fine wine to his lips when, from the chimney, he heard a thin, sad voice. "Oh me," the voice wailed. "Oh me! Oh me!"

Esteban swallowed his wine and carefully set the flask beside him. He leaned forward and said in his most cheerful way, "That's not a very happy greeting, my friend." Then with a fork he moved the bacon around in the pan so that all the sides would brown evenly. Again he breathed in the delicious smell. Then, looking towards the chimney, he said, "My friend, that sound you make is bearable enough to a man such as me who is accustomed to the braying of his donkey."

"Oh me," sobbed the voice once more. "Oh me! Oh me! Oh me!"

Esteban laid a piece of brown paper on a plate beside him and, with great precision, he lifted each piece of bacon from the pan. These he placed, one by one, on the paper so that the fat might drain, and he reached again into his pack and lifted out the eggs. He broke one into the sizzling fat and gently shook the pan so that the edges of his egg would cook up crisp and brown and the yolk would stay soft.

Then the voice came again. This time it was louder and higher, shrill and full of fear. "*Look out below*," called the voice, "*I'm falling.*"

"All right," Esteban said calmly, "only please don't fall into my frying pan."

At that he heard a loud thump and there on the hearth beside the frying pan lay a man's leg! It was a good enough leg, clothed in half a pair of fine corduroy trousers.

Esteban reached into the pan and took out his egg which was nicely crisp on the outside and soft and yellow in the centre, and this he ate with a slice of bacon, and he drank once again from his flask.

Outside the rain began to beat against the windows of the cold, haunted castle.

◆

Part Two

ESTEBAN MOVED CLOSER to the fire and took another swig of
wine when once again he heard, "*Look out below.*" And this time the
voice was even sharper. "*Look out below, I'm falling*!" And he heard
another thump!

There on the hearth lay a second leg clothed exactly like the first in
half a pair of fine corduroy trousers.

Esteban moved the leg away from the hearth so that he could pile on
more sticks and build up his fire which was beginning to die. He added
the sticks and again the flames leapt up golden red, and the room
grew warmer still, while outside the wind shrieked and the rain
pounded down. Then Esteban warmed the fat in his frying pan and
into this he broke a second egg.

"*Look out below!*" This time the voice was like a roar, a strong, lusty yell. "*Look out below, I'm falling!*"

Esteban looked up and smiled and yelled cheerfully back, "Fall away then," and he shook his pan and added, "only please don't fall into my egg."

And then there came a thump, louder and heavier than the first two thumps, and there on the hearth lay a trunk dressed in a starched white shirt and a corduroy coat that matched the trousers.

Esteban ate his second egg with a slice of bacon and a long swig of fine wine, and then he broke the third egg into the sizzling fat. He twirled the pan so that the egg would cook up just right. Then, lifting the egg from the pan he ate it.

Just as he was taking the last swallow, the voice called again, "*Look out below, I'm falling.*" Thump! Thump! And there on the hearth lay first one arm and then the other.

"Now," Esteban thought as he put the pan back on the fire and slipped more bacon into the fat, "there is only the head. And I confess, I am curious to see the head of this curious body."

And then the voice thundered, even louder than before, louder than a human voice, "*Look out below!*" The noise was so great that the walls shook with its force. "*Look out below, I'm falling!*"

And down the chimney tumbled a head!

As heads go, this was a good enough head. It had thick black hair and a long black beard and its eyes were dark, though they looked a little unhappy, strained and nervous.

Esteban's bacon was only half-cooked, but he took the pan from the fire and laid it aside. And just as he did that, he looked up and before his eyes he saw all the parts of the body move and join together. There in front of him stood a living man – or the living man's ghost – and if Esteban had not removed the pan from the fire even he might have burned his fingers on the hot pan, for the sight was surprising indeed!

Still, Esteban remained calm. "Good evening, sir," he said merrily. "Won't you have an egg and a bit of bacon?"

"I need no food," said the ghost. "But I will tell you something right here and now. You are the only man of all those who have come to this castle who would stay here until I could put my body back together again. All the others died of fright before I had half finished the chore."

"Well," said Esteban, "that is simply because they did not have sense enough to bring food with them." With that he turned back to his frying pan and moved to place it on the fire.

"Wait!" the ghost cried. "If only you would help me a bit more, you could save me altogether from this eternal wandering."

Esteban lowered the pan and listened.

"There are three bags buried outside in the courtyard beneath the cypress tree. One is full of copper coins, and one is full of silver and the third is full of gold. I stole these from thieves and I brought them here to the castle to hide them. But as soon as I had buried those bags, the thieves arrived and they murdered me and cut me up into pieces. Even so, they never did find the gold, silver and copper coins. If you come with me and dig them up, you can give the copper coins to the poor, and you can give the silver coins to the sick, and you can keep the gold coins for yourself. And then I will be free to leave this castle and rest at last."

Esteban thought this sounded like a fine idea, and so he went out into the courtyard with the ghost. The donkey saw them and began to bray like he never had, but Esteban ignored his animal and he and the ghost walked on towards the cypress tree. "Dig," the ghost said.

"Dig yourself," Esteban said to him.

So the ghost dug. After a long while he reached the three bags of coins. He bent down and lifted them out and turned again to Esteban. "Now," said the ghost, "do you promise you will do with these as I have asked?"

"Yes," Esteban said. "I promise."

"All right then," said the ghost. "Now strip my clothes from me."

Esteban did this, and as soon as he did, the ghost disappeared. Only his clothes remained there on the grass in the courtyard beneath the cypress tree.

Esteban carried the coins into the great hall of the castle, and there he fried another egg and finished his bacon. Then, feeling full and satisfied, he curled up before the blazing fire and went to sleep.

Early the next morning the village people climbed the hill to fetch Esteban's body. To their astonishment, when they entered the great hall, they saw the cheerful tinker sitting before the fire, cooking an omelette made from the last of the eggs.

"You are alive!" they gasped, amazed. They had all expected to find another lifeless body before the hearth in the haunted castle's great hall.

"I am," Esteban said calmly, "and the food and the sticks lasted me nicely through the night. Now I will go to the castle's owner to collect my reward. The ghost has gone for good, and you will find that his clothes are lying out in the courtyard beneath the cypress tree."

And then, before the astonished eyes of all the villagers, Esteban loaded the three bags of coins onto his donkey's back and rode down the hill.

First he went to the castle's master where he collected his thousand gold pieces from the grateful man. Then he returned to the city and gave the copper coins to the poor, and he distributed the silver coins to all the sick people, and with his reward and the golden coins from the third bag, he lived idly and contentedly for many, many years.

◆

Monkey Business

A Fable From India

◆

ONCE UPON A TIME, Mother Crocodile lived with her son in a great, wide river full of other crocodiles. And on the banks of that great, wide river there were huge, tall trees. And in those huge, tall trees lived dozens of little monkeys.

For a long, long time Mother Crocodile watched the monkeys. One day she said to her son, "Son, I want one of those monkeys. I want to eat the heart of a monkey. You must get me a monkey."

"But Mother," said Young Crocodile, "how am I to catch a monkey? Monkeys do not come into the water, and Crocodiles do not travel on land."

Mother Crocodile sighed deeply. "Use your wits," she said. "You will find a way."

Young Crocodile thought and thought and thought.

At last he knew what to do. "I'll get the monkey who lives in the tallest tree on the riverbank," Young Crocodile said to himself. "He likes to eat ripe fruit more than all the other monkeys and the best and most plentiful fruit is on the island in the middle of the river. To get it, Monkey would first have to cross the water."

So Young Crocodile swam across the river towards the tall tree where Monkey lived. "Oh, Monkey," cried Young Crocodile, "come with me to the island where the ripest fruit grows."

Monkey perched on the edge of a branch and looked down at Young Crocodile. "How can I go there? I do not swim."

"Ah," said Young Crocodile, "but I do. I will take you to the island on my back."

Monkey was greedy and wanted the ripest fruits to eat, and so he jumped from his tree onto Young Crocodile's back and off they went.

"This is a fine ride you're giving me," Monkey chattered. "A fine, very fine, fine ride."

Young Crocodile grinned. "You think so?" he asked. "What about this?" And he dived.

"No, no!" cried Monkey as they plunged beneath the smooth surface. Monkey was afraid to let go of Crocodile. He did not know what to do underwater.

Young Crocodile came up and Monkey sputtered and choked. "Crocodile, why did you take me underwater?" he coughed.

"To kill you," answered Young Crocodile. "My mother wants monkey heart to eat."

"Well," said Monkey, "I wish you had told me you wanted my heart. If you had told me I would have brought it with me."

"What?" cried Young Crocodile. "Do you mean to tell me that you left your heart in the trees back on the shore?"

"Yes," said Monkey. "If it is my heart you want we'll have to travel back to the tree to get it. But first, can't we please visit the island with the ripe fruit? We are so near."

"No, no," said Young Crocodile, "we must go straight back to the tree. Never mind about the fruit." And he swam back towards the river's edge towards the tree.

"Now," said Young Crocodile, "you get your heart and bring it back to me at once and then, perhaps, we'll visit the island."

"Very well," sighed Monkey, and he scrambled onto the bank of the river. Then, whoosh, he scampered up the tree.

And then, from the highest branches, Monkey called down to Young Crocodile who lay in the water below. "My heart is up here, Young Crocodile, and if you want it, you must come here and get it. Then perhaps we'll visit your mother!"

And with that, all the other little monkeys chattered and laughed away. But the saucy little monkey in the tallest tree, laughed the loudest and the longest – with all his heart, you might say.

◆

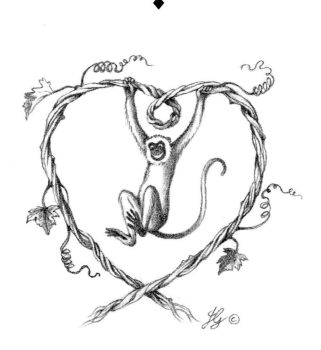

Why a Rabbit Lives on the Moon

A Japanese Tale Retold by Mary Beaty

◆

*Since time began, human beings have been watching
the moon. Its silvery presence fills us with wonder
as its shape seems to change
from a thin crescent to a full, round disk.
It signals the passing months, pulls the tides
and lights our way at night.
Legends about the moon are told in almost every country.
Some people look at the full moon and see
only shadows on its surface. Others imagine a man's face
while still others see a beautiful maiden.
In Japan, people look for the little rabbit who lives there.*

EVERY NIGHT THE Old Man in the Moon looked down upon the earth to see how the animals and people fared in the world below. One evening he saw Monkey, Fox and Rabbit all living together in the forest in friendship. Wondering which of the three friends was the kindest, he changed himself into a beggar and descended to earth to find out.

The beggar then wandered into the forest. When he reached the clearing where the three animals were, he leaned on his stick and said, "Please help me, kind friends. I am old and hungry."

The three animals quickly ran off in search of food for the poor beggar.

Monkey returned first with an armful of fruit. Fox caught a fat fish. But Rabbit could find nothing at all to offer the old man. "What shall I do?" he cried. "I have nothing to feed the poor beggar."

Then Rabbit turned to Monkey and Fox and said, "Please, brother Monkey, gather firewood for me. And Brother Fox, please build a big fire with the wood."

They both did as Rabbit asked and when the fire was burning brightly Rabbit said, "I do not have anything to give the poor beggar except myself. So I'll jump into this fire, and when I am cooked, please give me to the poor man to eat."

At that moment the beggar threw away his stick and cast off his cloak and stood up straight and tall. The animals were terrified, but the Old Man in the Moon said gently and quietly, "You see, Rabbit, I am more than a beggar. And I have seen that you are far more than a timid rabbit. Your kindness is beyond price. But you should learn never to harm yourself. I shall take you home to live with me where I can watch over you always."

So the Old Man in the Moon took Rabbit gently in his arms and carried him up to his home. And if you look carefully at the moon when it is full and bright, you can see Rabbit in the arms of the Old Man where he has lived safely for a very, very long time and lives there still.

The Cow on the Roof

A Tale Told in Wales

◆

*April 1, is All Fools' Day, a day of mischief
and laughter, a day to play jokes on people.
How it started is not quite clear.
Some say it goes as far back as Noah and his ark!
This is the story of one very foolish man
who thought he was best at everything. Of course,
his wife knew better, and though it may not have been April 1,
she made sure the joke was on him.*

ONCE UPON A TIME there was a man who grumbled and griped that his wife could do nothing right. He complained about her cooking and the way she cleaned the house – in fact, about the way she did most everything. At last the wife grew tired of his grumbles and she told him she was going out to weed the turnips while he could stay home and mind the house. Her husband soon agreed to the plan, for he was sure that he would set her a fine example.

Out she went, saying as she departed, "Now, take care of the baby, slop the pig, feed the hens, turn the cow out to pasture, sweep the floor and dust the shelves. And make sure my supper is ready by the time I return." Then off she went to the fields while her husband stayed in the house.

The baby woke and began to weep and weep. The man rocked her cradle, and he sang to her, and rocked the cradle once again, but no matter what he did, the child wept and wept. Then the pig began to squeal in its pen, and the man got up to get some milk to make its food. But as he carried the bucket out of the house, he tipped it over and the milk spilled all over the floor. The pig, hearing the crash of the bucket, began to squeal more loudly, and the baby continued to cry.

The poor man could stand the racket no longer. He rushed out to its pen. "Find your food yourself!" he shouted to the pig as he opened the gate to turn the animal out.

The pig ran between his legs and the man fell into a dunghill. He got up, scraped the dirt from his clothes, and when he looked up, the pig was nowhere to be seen. When he went back into the house he saw the pig lapping up the milk he had spilled on the floor. In her haste to reach it, the pig had overthrown another bucket too.

"You rascal!" he cried, and grabbing up a piece of firewood, he gave the pig a whack. The pig wobbled and fell to the floor in a daze.

By then it was getting late, and the husband remembered his wife's supper, and he remembered that he had to turn the cow out to pasture, and he remembered that there were the hens to feed. The pasture was some distance away, and he was afraid that if he travelled all the way there with the cow he would not return home in time to make supper. And then he remembered that there was some fine grass growing on the roof of the house, which was thatched with sod. At the back of the house there was a rise up to the roof, and the roof reached almost to the top of the rise. "The roof," thought the man. "That would be a fine place for the cow to graze for just one day."

So the man walked outside and tied one end of the rope to the cow's halter and holding the other end, he ran up the roof. He dropped the other end of the rope down the chimney. Then, climbing down again, he went inside to cook his wife's supper. So that his hands might be free, he tied the end of the rope he had dropped down the chimney round his ankle.

He felt very clever indeed, that is, until he remembered the hens. He couldn't possibly leave the house now, since the cow was on the roof and its rope was tied to his ankle.

In the meantime, the cow had walked carefully up the roof, but when she came to the top and bent her head to graze, she slipped over the other side. The man felt the rope go tight, and up into the chimney he

went, feet first. But he did not fly all the way up, for his legs got caught upon the iron bar from which the porridge kettle hung. And there he stuck for what seemed a very long time. And all the while the poor baby wept, the cow bawled, the pig snored and the hens clucked for their feed.

Just then, and luckily too, his wife returned from the fields. The first thing she saw was the cow struggling in the air high above her. She ran to the door, and stepping inside she found the pig lying in a puddle of spilled milk. She picked up an axe and quickly moved to cut the rope to save the cow. But when she ran back inside, there was her husband, standing on his head in a kettle full of porridge as the baby cried and cried!

The wife looked at her husband, and she looked at the ruined porridge. Then she looked at the dazed pig, and she looked at the spilled milk, and she heard the chickens clucking in the distance. She picked up the baby and rocked her and sang sweetly to her and at last the baby fell peacefully to sleep.

The wife went on singing. "I had a fine day in the fields. The sun was warm and the air was fresh and now there is not one weed left amongst the turnips."

Then the pig, shaking itself awake, stood up and began again to lap the spilled milk. And the cow, safely on the ground outside, began to moo delightedly. The wife gently put the baby down and moved to the door to scatter some feed for the hens. Only after that did she help her husband out of the porridge kettle. When he was free, he stood up and looked at his wife and his wife looked back at him.

"I can see you've had a fine day too. It's a pity my supper isn't ready, though," laughed the wife, as she wiped porridge from her husband's face. And the husband, feeling every inch the fool, laughed with her.

◆

Fair, Brown
and Trembling

A Tale From Erin

◆

This Celtic tale adapted from Joseph Jacobs,
is one that may sound very familiar to you.
The well-loved story of Cinderella
has been told for so long and in so many countries
that its origins are cloudy. But the similarities
and differences between Cinderella and Fair, Brown and Trembling
are crystal clear.

Part One

THERE ONCE WERE three sisters who lived in Erin, and their names were Fair, Brown and Trembling.

Fair and Brown had new dresses and went to church every Sunday. Trembling, the youngest, stayed at home to do the cooking and other chores. Fair and Brown would not let her go out of the house at all for she was more beautiful than they. The two older sisters were afraid that Trembling might marry before they did.

For seven years they carried on in this way, and at the end of seven years the son of the king of Erin fell in love with Fair.

One Sunday morning, after Fair and Brown had gone to church, an old woman came to the kitchen door and said to Trembling, "It's at church you ought to be this day, instead of working here at home."

"How could I go?" said Trembling. "I have no clothes good enough to wear to church. And if my sisters were to see me there, they'd be furious with me for going out of the house."

"I'll give you a finer dress than either of them has ever seen, Trembling, dear," said the old woman. "And now tell me, what dress you would like?"

"I would like a dress as white as snow, and green shoes for my feet," Trembling said.

With that old woman put on her cloak – the cloak of darkness, she called it – clipped a piece of material from Trembling's ragged dress, and asked for the whitest, most beautiful robe in the world, with a pair of green shoes to go with it.

The moment she had the robe and the shoes, she gave them to Trembling who put them on. When Trembling was dressed and ready, the old woman said, "I have a honey-bird here to sit on your right shoulder, and a honey-finger to put on your left. Look out the door. There is a milk-white mare, with a golden saddle for you to sit on, and a golden bridle to hold in your hand."

Trembling climbed up into the golden saddle, and when she was ready to start, the old woman said to her, "You must go only to the door of the church, and the minute the people rise up at the end of Mass, you must make off, and ride home as fast as the mare will carry you."

As Trembling stood at the door of the church everyone who caught a glimpse of her wanted to know who she was, and when they saw her hurrying away at the end of Mass, they ran out to overtake her. But it was no use for she was away before anyone could come near her. From the minute she left the church till she got home, she overtook the wind before her and outstripped the wind behind.

She rushed inside to find the old woman had prepared dinner.

Trembling slipped out of her white robe and had on her old dress in a twinkling.

When the two sisters came home the old woman was gone and Trembling asked, "Have you any news today from the church?"

"We have great news," they said. "We saw a wonderful, grand lady at the church door. She wore robes such as we have never seen before. Our dresses were nothing compared to the one she wore, and there wasn't a man at the church, from king to beggar, who wasn't trying to look at her and know who she was."

Fair and Brown would not be still until they had two dresses as magnificent as the robes of the stranger. But search as they would, they could find no honey-birds or honey-fingers to wear upon their shoulders.

Next Sunday, Fair and Brown went to church again and left their sister Trembling at home to prepare their dinner. After they had gone, the old woman reappeared at the kitchen door and asked, "Will you go to church today, Trembling, dear?"

"I would go," said Trembling, "if I could."

"What robe would you wish to wear?" asked the woman.

"The finest black satin gown that could be found, and red shoes for my feet."

"What colour do you want the mare to be?"

"I want her to be so black and so glossy that I can see myself in her body."

The old woman's eyes twinkled as she put on the cloak of darkness, and asked for the robes and the shoes and the mare. In an instant she had them. When Trembling was dressed, the old woman put the honey-bird on her right shoulder and the honey-finger on her left. The saddle on the mare was silver, and so was the bridle.

Just when Trembling was about to gallop away, the woman called to her and once again warned her strictly not to go inside the door of the church, and to rush away as soon as the people rose at the end of Mass. "Hurry home on the mare before anyone can stop you," she called after Trembling.

That Sunday the people were more astonished than ever, and they gazed at Trembling more than they had the first time. They all were thinking only of how to find out who she was. But once again they had no chance, for the moment they rose at the end of Mass, Trembling slipped away and was in the silver saddle and home before anyone could stop her or talk to her.

Once again, the old woman had dinner ready. Once again, Trembling took off her beautiful clothes and put on her old dress. And once again, the old woman was safely away before the two sisters returned home.

"What news have you today?" asked Trembling of Fair and Brown when they returned.

"Oh, we saw the grand lady again. And it's little that any man could think of our dresses after looking at the satin robes that she wore! And all at church, from high to low, had their mouths open, gazing at her, and no man was looking at us."

The two sisters had neither rest nor peace till they got dresses of satin like the mysterious lady's robes. Of course, their dresses were not half so good, for in all of Erin there was no satin so fine.

When the third Sunday came, Fair and Brown went to church dressed in black satin. They left Trembling at home to work in the kitchen, and told her to be sure to have dinner ready when they came back.

After they had gone and were out of sight, the old woman came again to the kitchen door and said to Trembling, "Well, my dear, are you for church today?"

And Trembling smiled and said, "You know I would go, if I had a new dress to wear." And now Trembling knew what would happen next.

"I'll get you any dress you ask for. What dress would you like?"

"A dress as red as a rose from the waist down, and white as snow from the waist up; a cape of green on my shoulders; and for my head a hat with one red, one white, and one green feather in it; and shoes for my feet with red toes, white middles, and green backs and heels."

The old woman put on the cloak of darkness and wished for all these things. In a moment Trembling was dressed with the honey-bird on her right shoulder and the honey-finger on her left. Then placing the hat on the girl's head, the old woman clipped a few locks of Trembling's hair with her scissors, and instantly the most beautiful golden hair flowed over the girl's shoulders. Then the woman asked what kind of mare Trembling would ride. She asked for a white horse, with blue and gold-coloured diamond-shaped markings all over her body. For the mare's back Trembling asked for a saddle of gold, and for her head, a golden bridle.

The mare stood there before the door just as Trembling had described her, but with one added touch. Sitting between her ears was a bird which began to sing as soon as Trembling was in the saddle. And the bird never stopped its song till Trembling returned home from church.

The fame of the beautiful stranger had spread across the land, and all the princes and great men came to church that third Sunday, each one hoping that he could ask her home with him after Mass.

The prince of Erin, the very one who had once loved Fair, had by now forgotten all about his affection for her. He remained outside the church so that he might stop the mysterious lady before she could hurry away.

The church was more crowded than ever before, and there were three times as many people gathered outside. There was such a throng in the church yard that Trembling could only come inside the gate.

As soon as the people began to rise at the end of Mass, Trembling hurried out through the gate, jumped into the golden saddle and swept away, ahead of the wind. But this time the prince of Erin was at her side, and seizing her by the foot, he ran with the mare for thirty paces and never let go of Trembling until her shoe came off. And there he stood, left behind, with nothing for his effort but the shoe in his hand.

Trembling rushed home as fast as the mare could carry her, thinking all the time that the old woman would be angry that she had lost her shoe.

Seeing her so flustered and worried, the woman asked, "What's the trouble, Trembling? What's on you now?"

"Oh! One of the shoes was torn from my foot by a handsome prince as I dashed away after Mass," said Trembling.

"Don't mind that," the old woman soothed. "Maybe it's the best thing that ever happened to you."

Trembling put on her old clothes and went to work in the kitchen.

When Fair and Brown came home, she asked, "Have you any news from the church?"

"We have indeed," said they, "for we saw the grandest sight today. The strange lady came again, in finer array than before. On herself and the horse were the brightest colours in the world, and between the ears of the horse was a bird which never stopped singing from the time she came till she went away. The lady herself is the most beautiful woman ever seen by the people of Erin."

◆

Part Two

AFTER TREMBLING HAD disappeared from the church, the son of the king of Erin said to the other kings' sons: "I love that lady and will ask her to be my wife."

They all said, "You didn't win her just by taking the shoe off her foot. You'll have to win her by the point of the sword for we love her too. You'll have to fight with us before you can ask her to wed."

"Well," said the prince, "I will find the lady that shoe fits. And I'll fight for her, never fear, before I leave her to any of you."

Then all the kings' sons were uneasy and anxious to know who it was who had lost her shoe. The prince of Erin and all the others began to travel the whole of Erin to find her. They went north, south, east, and west. They visited every place where a woman was to be found, and there was not a house in the kingdom they did not search. They searched only for the woman whose foot would fit that shoe, not caring whether she was rich or poor, of high or low degree.

The prince of Erin always kept the shoe, and when the young women saw it, they had great hopes, for it was of proper size, neither large nor small. One woman thought it would fit her if she cut a little from her great toe. Another, with too short a foot, put something in the tip of her stocking. But it was no use. The women only spoiled their feet, and for months afterwards spent their days curing them.

Fair and Brown heard that the princes of the world were looking all over Erin for the woman that could wear the shoe, and every day they talked of trying it on.

One day Trembling spoke up and said, "Maybe it's my foot that the shoe will fit."

"Oh, the breaking of the dog's foot on you! Why say so when you were at home every Sunday?"

They went on that way, scolding their youngest sister till the princes were near the place. The day they were to come, Fair and Brown put Trembling in a closet and locked the door on her. When the company came to the house, the prince of Erin gave the shoe to Fair and then to Brown. But though they tried and tried it, it fit neither of them.

"Is there any other young woman in the house?" asked the prince.

"There is," said Trembling, speaking up from the closet. "I'm here."

"Oh! She is good for nothing but to put out the ashes," said Fair and Brown.

But the prince and the others wouldn't leave the house till they had seen Trembling. So at last, Fair and Brown had to open the door. When Trembling came out the shoe was given to her, and it fit exactly.

The prince of Erin looked at her and said, "You are the woman the shoe fits, and you are the woman I took the shoe from."

Then Trembling spoke up and said, "Stay here till I return."

Trembling ran down the road, straight to the old woman's cottage. When the old woman heard that the prince was waiting, she put on the cloak of darkness. In an instant everything from that first Sunday was there. The old woman dressed Trembling in the white robes and put her on the white mare in the same fashion. Then Trembling rode along the highway to the front of the house. All who had seen her the first Sunday said, "This is the lady we saw at church."

Then Trembling went away a second time, and a second time came back on the black mare, dressed in the black satin which the old woman had given her. All who had seen her the second Sunday said, "That is the lady we saw at church."

A third time she asked for a short absence and soon came back on the third mare and in the third dress. All who had seen her the third time said, "That is the lady we saw at church." Now everyone was satisfied and knew that she was indeed the woman.

Then all the jealous princes said to the son of the king of Erin, "You'll have to fight now for the lady before we let you ask her for her hand in marriage."

"I'm here before you, ready for combat," answered the prince.

Then the son of the king of Lochlin stepped forth. The struggle began, and a terrible struggle it was. They fought for nine hours. And then the son of the king of Lochlin stopped, gave up his claim, and left the field. Next day the son of the king of Spain fought six hours, and at last yielded his claim. On the third day the son of the king of Nyerfoi fought eight hours, and yielded. The fourth day the son of the king of Greece fought six hours, and stopped. By the fifth day there were no more princes brave enough to fight.

And so at last, the prince of Erin had won his right to ask Trembling for her hand in marriage. Of course, she agreed and the marriage-day was fixed, and the invitations were sent out. The wedding was the most glorious one ever seen in the land. Among all the grand guests sat an old woman dressed in a dark cloak. And beside her sat the sisters, Fair and Brown. Even they, in the presence of so many grand folk and so many fine princes, had a wonderful day and were happy for their sister's happiness.